Hopeless Magic

Hopeless Magic

A.K. Koonce

To the Hopeless. May they return to us and save us all.

Table of Contents

Chapter One

The White Light

Coarse strands of rope twist through my fingers as I haul myself even higher up the tower. My fingers thread right through it and I realize the rope hanging from the window isn't a rope at all but … human hair.

The night wind whips cruelly against me, pushing my small frame against the side of the disintegrating brick wall. My pale locks sting across my cheeks. I clench my jaw and lift my gaze higher to the window with the blinking light. It's unnatural. The white light burns brightly into the dark sky before fading into nothingness.

I heave another breath as my boots shift against the wall and I pull myself up the ancient tower. Rocks scrape and crumble beneath my every move, falling away with ease. A stinging numbness sets into my thin fingers and I'm starting to wish I had

1

stolen that drunk's coat before I left the bar.

The way he spoke about the unseen tower miles out of town, the tales he told of the wealth that rests within it, had my feet moving before he'd even slurred a word of warning.

No one's ever been able to warn me of anything, though. So what if I'm an orphan? So what if I'm not tall enough or strong enough? So what if I'm a girl? So what if I'm too pretty to be taken seriously?

That's never stopped me before, and it certainly isn't going to stop me from claiming the prize at the top of this fortress.

Solid brick greets my nails as I dig into the opening of the window. A burning breath stings my lungs. I throw my leg over the ledge and slip inside without a sound.

The light's gone now. Darkness veils my sight. The long hair that lead me up the tower is tied off on a rusting hook. Next to the hook is something white. Something familiar. Something that makes my skin crawl just looking at it.

A human skull.

I turn away, rejecting the sight of it. My shoulders square and I pull the sword from my belt.

The weight of it settles my nerves. It was my father's. Before I was a thief, I was just a pretty little girl with a promising future ahead of her. After my father's death was when I learned all the things that made me the resilient woman I am today.

His blade helped mold me even without his presence.

Something in the shadows shifts, my gaze sweeps every inch of the dark room.

"You should leave. Now," a deep voice warns. But he's too late.

A short dagger glints in the moonlight. I barely have time to see the shine of it before it quickly sinks into my side.

Horrified gasps part my lips and my brows pull together in anger and confusion.

The attacker slips the dagger from my flesh as quickly as it came. My fingers slide slickly across my skin as I press hard against the wound.

Hot blood pools through my fingertips. My heart thrashes in my chest and I just know.

It's fatal.

Painfully, my jaw clenches as a scarred and

twisting face reveals itself to me.

"You should have listened to our little Prince, love." His gruff voice crawls through the small room. Shadows hide his features from me, but he tilts his head to the corner of the room at the mention of *our little Prince.*

I breathe hard before raising my father's sword with more strength than I intend. I plunge it into the man, railing it through his abdomen. I don't stop until it's all the way through his wide body, clinking against the brick wall behind him.

His glossy eyes hold mine, and my lips purse firmly as I hold his stare.

It's a look that screams *fuck off.* It's a look I usually reserve for clingy boyfriends, but I suppose it works here as well.

Even as I bleed out, I'll cling to that false sense of strength I always seem to hold.

I don't have the energy to retrieve the blade from his frame as he sinks to the floor with a solid thud. My vision blurs, my breaths becoming shorter and shorter. It's an effort just to take shallow gasps of air.

I've seen death enter a man's eyes before with a vacant and fearful shine. I've seen his life slip through his fingertips.

It won't be long now …

"Get the key," someone whispers. His voice circles the room.

As I stand here dying someone seems to think they have something more important to be doing. My death seems to really be interfering with their fabulous day.

The white light I saw from the woods, the white light that lead me here to my death, it strikes through the room once more. It flickers sporadically, waning into a dim hue of gold.

Three men stand gripping the bars of a jail cell in the corner of the room. The one with golden hair holds his hands together as if he's harnessing a force between his palms. The light burns with a pulsing hue from the center of his hands.

What is he holding?

"Come on, we've been here for over a year, love. Get the key."

A shaking breath filled with annoyance parts my dry lips.

"Did you see what happened to the last man that called me *love*?" I narrow my eyes on the prisoner with the pale gray gaze. My lips twist with confidence even though I feel my strength fading.

The other man at his side turns to him with a smirk pulling at his features. There's a similarity between the two men. One holds taunting humor and the other total anger. It's then that I realize they're the same.

They're twins.

"Please, lo—*woman*, get the key." Yes, because women love nothing more than to be called affectionately by their gender.

Asshole.

The scowl never leaves his handsome, dirty face as he points across the room to a single key displayed proudly in a glass case. A dim light illuminates the key, taunting them with the closeness of their freedom.

The scraping sound of my boots moving sluggishly skims through the small room. I lean into the wall as I reach high for the brass key.

The thin display case teeters and the enclosing box falls away from the key. Fine particles of glass shatter across my boots but I don't notice it as I stand on the tips of my toes to reach the key. It's cold against my skin. My fingerless leather gloves are all that separates its metal from my numbing flesh.

I turn back to them and the three stand wide-eyed, watching me with expectation as I hold their lives in my hands.

Over the years, I've been taught to never give anything away for free. A person's life is worth quite a bit.

I know because mine's already gone.

Panic wraps itself tightly around my stomach as I realize I can't manage a real intake of air. I push aside the selfish thought and walk to them with fear gripping my chest. My life is over, but their lives don't have to be. The key fits perfectly into the lock with a scraping sound of metal on metal. It turns with ease.

One of the twins claps his hands as they all race from the cell.

My eyes close heavily and I sink to the floor in a warm puddle of my own blood. Slick fingers fall from the fatal puncture wound, my hands no longer able to hold the life within me.

The man with dark hair, one of the twins, lowers himself down to his knees. Crimson blood stains his dirty jeans.

He clings tightly to a mysterious light in his hands.

"Thank you," he says. My eyes flutter, wanting to see him—the last person who will ever see me before I die.

I guess I won't die alone after all.

The effort of opening my eyes is too much.

He presses a warm kiss to my temple. It's an affectionate gesture that I would have hated if I weren't teetering on the hazy line between life and death. It feels nice, though. To feel loved. To feel treasured. To feel ... like my life mattered.

Even if it is just pretend.

A painful, empty breath shakes from my lungs, the last one I have the strength to take.

Heat radiates through my side as he presses his hand to my flesh, just over the knife wound. A light shines brightly against my closed lids. Nerves tingle all through my body.

A strong sound pounds loudly through my ears, filling my hazy consciousness.

My heartbeat.

Chapter Two
Hopeless

My eyes flutter open. Moonlight shines down on me, casting the tree limbs of the forest into a disarray of tangled shadows.

For a moment, an odd dream drifts through my mind. A dream I've had a time or two before; a dream of my death.

It felt real this time.

"Hey, she's awake."

My eyes flutter open and I realize I'm snuggled against a man's chest. Even worse, I just ran my fingers up his hard pecs in appreciation.

The only thing that could seal my ridiculousness is a slow hum of approval.

So I do just that. A lazy moan of affection parts my lips and I settle my head comfortably onto his shoulder. Then I fling my eyes wide open, pushing the sleep from my mind to remind myself this is real life and I cannot stroke strangers I do not know.

What is wrong with me?

I jerk my hand back from him as if he's on fire and I don't want to have the misfortune of joining him in the flames.

Shoving hard, I push out of his capable arms. My feet hit the dry forest floor with ease and I turn to him as my hand moves to my belt. Nothing but smooth leather greets my fingertips. The cold, hard metal of my sword is nowhere to be found.

I stumble back, fear threading through my veins as I realize I don't have the weapon I always depend on. My back hits something solid and I turn, coming face to face with the lightest blue eyes I've ever seen. It's like looking into the pale early morning sky.

"Looking for this?" the man asks with a gleam in his bright gaze. He holds my father's sword in his grubby hands, a scornful smirk lacing his full lips.

Tightly, my mouth closes, my jaw setting hard as I glare up at his impressive height. It takes less than a second for me to assess my situation.

The two men, who appear to be twins, stand carelessly behind me. Neither of them move in to harm me. Neither of them appear to be a threat.

The man before me is the only one who seems to pose a threat since he holds my sword. But it's a playful look that fills his features. Stains of dirt tarnish his white shirt that's pulled tight against his broad shoulders.

They're all too large for me to really defend myself against.

And that thought alone decides their unfortunate fates.

With a swift jerk of my leg, my knee meets his balls. I reach for my darling sword just as he drops it, his wide shoulders hulking down as he holds his most precious possession.

"Didn't expect that," one of them says casually from behind me.

The twins exchange a surprised look and I don't give them any warning before I dart off into the night.

"Get her. We need her!"

Fear snaps through my chest as I push my feet to move faster. Twigs crack beneath my hurried steps, and limbs lash across my flesh. None of it registers in my mind.

My life is all I care about. Surviving is all I've ever known. Tomorrow's mine for the taking, as my father always said. That phrase holds a new meaning now that I'm older. Tomorrow will come. I'll be there to see it. Tomorrow's mine for the taking, as long as I can survive today.

My boots stumble against slick mud and my breath catches as his body slams into mine. I thrash against his strong embrace, my hair flicking across my face as I struggle. Warmth seeps into me from his body against mine. It's an overwhelming warmth that makes it difficult to breathe.

"Get off of me." I stomp hard on his boot but he doesn't release his hold. "You'll regret ever laying a hand on me." My voice teeters into an angry shriek that echoes into the night.

I sound like a pissed off little girl. I probably look like a pissed off little girl the way he's holding me as if I'm a thrashing toddler.

"Calm down, human." His voice is gravelly and rumbles through his chest.

He turns us, still holding me firmly from behind.

In all my life, no one's ever held me like this. No one's ever gotten the upper hand on me.

"Darrio, shit, you're scaring the hell out of her. Let her go already." The man with identical features to my captor gives him an impatient look, his brow raising as he studies us. "You two look cute like that, by the way."

"Shut up, Daxdyn," Darrio says in a gruff voice.

His twin smirks at him, seeming pleased that he got under his brother's skin so easily.

"Both of you knock it off. We need her."

Calm breaths meet my lungs as I force the adrenaline building in me to a dull hum.

"What do you want?" I ask in a sharp but reasonable tone.

The blonde, the one I just introduced my knee to, gives me an odd look.

"You got a lot of fight in you for someone who nearly died an hour ago," he tells me.

My lips part. Nothing but a surprised breath escapes.

He's lying. It doesn't stop the doubt from

circling my mind, though.

"What do you want?" I stiffen my spine to my full height, my body going rigid in Darrio's arms. Out of the corner of my eye I can see his dark beard pressed against the top of my head.

Thin lines slash up and down the bronze forearms wrapped around me. Scars kiss his skin; the scars of a man who's seen battle too many times it appears. My attention lingers there for a moment before staring up at the men in front of me.

"We need you to take us somewhere," the blonde tells me hesitantly. "We were drugged and captured over a year ago and we need to get home. We don't even know where we are."

Does he expect me to feel bad for him?

"And why would I help you?" I pause, my brow arching high, "*Again.*"

Darrio shifts until his dark hair can be seen. I turn to him and he narrows his gray eyes at me. "Do you really feel you're in the right position to be sounding so condescending?" His words are gruff and clipped, and the way his voice sounds almost holds my attention for a moment. It's a voice you feel everywhere on your body; an

14

alluring sound that you want to hear as a whisper against your neck.

Swiftly, I shake the thought from my head.

I roll my eyes at him and the other two men smile back at me.

The man with short, light hair takes a few steps closer to me. His hand reaches up and he pushes back my long, tangled hair with ease. My teeth clench together painfully as I shake my hair away from his touch.

"We did save your life. Isn't that reason enough?" he asks.

A tingling feeling races through my body and my fingers twitch at my side with the memory of the dagger sinking into my flesh.

Was that real?

I push the strange memory away. My shoulders square and I cling to my confidence.

"You'll have to do better than that; my life isn't worth very much." My lips quirk into a smile I don't feel.

"I like her," Daxdyn says with a smirk that warms his eyes.

"You like everyone," Darrio replies in an even tone.

"Her especially." Daxdyn gives me a wink that makes him too attractive for his own good. He's all smooth features and even smoother talk.

I've met a thousand men like him in my life. His charming swagger will get him killed one day. I'd bet money on it.

"I can pay you," the blonde finally tells me. He folds his arms securely across his broad chest.

"Hmm a prisoner paying a thief. Sound's reliable." Sarcasm drenches my words. I stand before him unflinching as he assesses me from head to toe.

"You're a thief?"

The cold wind chills my flesh, whipping at the exposed skin of my lean abdomen. My dark jeans are ripped and worn. The stolen weapon's belt at my hips is too large and is disheveled from my struggle with Darrio.

I'm a mess.

A beautiful fucking mess.

Daxdyn's gaze trails across my body as well, heating my flesh with his burning attention.

"You're too pretty to be a thief."

"I'm not too pretty to save your ass, though, am I?"

A beat passes as we just stare at one another. He smirks at me with a gleaming look of happiness in his silver eyes. Daxdyn holds a confidence that probably makes women crazy. One that makes them do stupid, stupid things just for his affection. All his smile does is set me on edge. I'm certain I'm the only female on the planet who's complaining about his good looks.

"Have you ever heard the term, *Rich and Hopeless*?"

The Hopeless; a fae fairytale that I've heard since I was a child.

Fae magic used to fuel our world. It burned through it, brought it to life the way technology once did.

Until it slowly dwindled off. Leaving us behind with a burnt-up aftertaste of what we once had. No one's held power like that in decades—since before I was born.

Some believe the fae still exist. That they're hiding from the mortals who used and abused them. But I know for a fact it isn't true. It's a hopeless belief and filled with hopeless dreams.

The Hopeless fae.

It's said that the last remaining fae are richer than our wildest dreams. Supply and demand. They have a supply of something that's very high in demand.

"What about it?"

"Call me Hopeless, beautiful." A smile slashes across his face.

My eyes narrow on him and his insinuation. The blonde isn't delicate and full of beauty. The man holding me definitely isn't. Fae are said to be the most beautiful beings who ever graced this terrible world.

The other man, the one with the ever-present smile, almost fits the description.

But not the one who seems to be their leader. He isn't anything like the fae my father used to read me stories of.

"You're lying."

It's then that I realize Darrio isn't clinging to me like his life depends on it. His arms are held loosely around my frame, his body leaning into mine. And for some strange reason I allow it. A feeling swirls through me as I lean back on him too.

It's an intimate stance, his body wrapped around mine. No one's ever held me like this ...

Darrio's breathing halts for a moment. His corded arms tighten their hold on me once more.

Ah, there's the brooding brute again.

"You think I'm a liar?" the blonde man with the boyish good looks asks.

I raise an eyebrow at him, my lips set in a thin line.

Slowly, he pushes up the sleeve of his shirt. The white fabric bunches at the elbow and trailing down his forearm are black markings.

Angled lines of raised ink mar his flesh all the way to the wrist. The markings are upraised abnormally, as if something beneath the skin is pushing to get out.

The mark of the Hopeless.

I swallow hard and slowly my eyes meet his.

Daxdyn steps forward, the moonlight filtering across his beautiful face.

He, too, pushes up the sleeve of his left arm.

An identical mark skims across his flesh.

Darrio releases me and, hesitantly, I turn to him.

While his brother holds a face of perfection, Darrio's body is lined with flaws. A lifetime of battle slices through his flesh. Not an inch of skin is untouched. Long, tangled locks are pulled back from his face. A dark beard shadows his face, making him appear even more untamed.

And yet, he sets a tingle of nervous energy spiraling through my body at the serious look he holds in his beautiful eyes.

My gaze falls to his arms as he begins to turn his wrist to reveal what I already know is there.

The mark of the Hopeless scars them all.

Chapter Three

Liars

"Take us to the city," the blonde says, my attention still drifting to the marking against his left arm.

"I can't. The City of the Hopeless is a myth. It does not exist." My clipped words are harsh as I try to convince even myself. I'm not friendly and I'm not going to pretend to be for anyone. Even the supposed Hopeless.

"Take us to the Juvar Kingdom then."

Confusion swirls through me and I fold my arms across my chest.

"It's near Juvar?"

A smile tilts his arrogant lips. Gods above, does his smile make me want to give him anything he asks for. I avert my eyes. I don't fold that easily.

Usually.

"You sound very interested for someone who doesn't believe me."

I grind my teeth, refusing to give into his banter.

"Let's say I take you to Juvar. What will you give me?" A dirty thought crosses my mind as I appraise the way his shirt clings to his hard chest.

He licks his lips slowly, the smile growing larger.

"Whatever you like. Name your price," he says it in a slow, sexy tone as if my price is fueled by lust.

Not a chance.

Money fuels me. Adrenaline spikes through me like I have the money in my hands already.

"What's your name?" I ask him.

"Prince Ryder." He extends his hand to me and the twins exchange a knowing look. Their appearances are similar but their thoughts seem to be identical.

My attention shifts between the three of them suspiciously.

"*Prince*?"

Prince Ryder bites his cheek, biting back the sexy smile that kisses his lips.

"Before I was a Hopeless fae, I was the son of the King of Juvar. I'm the exiled Prince of Juvar."

The word 'exiled' stands out among all others. I bite my lower lip, my fingers thrumming against the smooth hilt of my sword at my hip.

How much money could a former prince really have? How much magic would a supposed Hopeless have?

Darrio places his hand on my wrist, holding it. His palm is rough against my skin. My gaze drifts from his grip on me to his steely eyes.

"You're not really in a place to be *considering* his offer." His hand tightens on mine.

"If you do not stop *manhandling* me, you'll regret it."

It's probably not the smartest thing in the world to be threatening someone who may or may not have enough power to murder me without lifting a finger.

He shakes his head. My eyes flutter closed and a long sigh falls from my lips.

Why does everyone doubt me?

I warned him he would regret it. I gave him two chances. And yet, he continues to test me.

The dagger strapped to my outer leg is in my palm in an instant. Within another two seconds, I've jammed it hard into the top of his thigh.

A growling groan pushes through his clenched teeth, but it's a reserved, smothered sound of pain. Every muscle in his body tenses.

"Fuck, she tried to warn you," Daxdyn says with laughter singing through his tone.

Suddenly, I like Daxdyn a little more.

Each finger slowly lifts from my hand and Darrio holds my blazing gaze as he fists the hilt. With a jarring move, he rips it from his thigh. His eyes close; the only sign of discomfort he gives.

My brow rises high. I'm slightly impressed and even more than slightly attracted to the new stranger I just met.

I must be a fucking masochist.

Without hesitation, I lift my hand, extending my palm out to him.

His jaw tics and he shifts his weight to his good leg before placing the dagger in my palm.

"Thanks." I give him a warm smile before turning my back on him; confident he won't touch me ever again. Ryder's charming smile is still on display. He glances toward Darrio before giving me his full attention. The line between my shoulders keeps an appearance of assuredness held in my posture. "I want an exchange."

Ryder's smile grows wolfish. He shoves his hands into his pockets and nods to me. "Everyone has a Hopeless price."

I nearly roll my eyes once more at the way he's throwing this hopeless word into every hopeless thing he says. It's not the f-word. It doesn't transition that hopeless way ... fuck, maybe it does.

"If," I pause on the word, letting it ring out with clarity, "I take you to the kingdom," with precision, I wipe Darrio's blood from my blade onto my dusty black jeans. I take my time, drawing out the anticipation of what I'm about to say, "I want a Hopeless exchange. I want something only magic can give me."

"What do you want?" He looks me up and down. His gaze drifts down my long legs before coming back up to my narrowed, green eyes.

My head tilts just minimally.

I don't know these men. I definitely don't trust them. I refuse to give them information after only knowing them for less than a day.

"I'll name my price once we come to the ocean that leads to the island of Juvar." Daxdyn shoots Ryder a look. They'd be stupid to agree to an open trade where I could ask for anything I like. But he nods anyway. What an idiot.

"What's your name?" Ryder nods to me.

The countless fake names I've used over the last five years threaten to slip across my tongue. I choke the names back though. For some strange reason, I don't lie to him.

"Zakara Storm." The three of them eye one another, the gazes shifting over my head to each other.

They're probably wondering if I made it up.

If I made it up, it'd be something prettier and more appealing to say. Maybe Angela or Jenée, or even Nicole. Not something that sounds like a fucking angry sneeze.

"How old are you, Zakara?" Even the way he says my name comes out in a mocking tone, a disbelieving sound.

"Twenty-one," I say in a flat voice.

Ryder's probably just a few years older than myself. Depending on how fae age, I suppose. And the twins are a total mystery. Darrio looks to be the oldest of the three. Even the way he holds himself makes him seem older with worn confidence, and yet Daxdyn appears younger than even myself. Smooth, boyish skin and a glimmering light in his eyes make him appear barely eighteen.

A long sigh parts my lips. I won't bother asking their age. It makes no difference if they're eighteen or one hundred and eighteen.

I slip the blade back into the tattered leather sheath on my outer thigh. A wide tree supports Ryder's weight as he leans into it, his hands still pushed into his pockets. He holds a careless posture. Not anything like I would imagine from a man of royalty.

"You're a prince. How do you not know the way home?" I ask, changing the subject.

The cold bites into my skin and I hug my arms around myself. None of them seem to be aware of the chilly temperature.

"When my scars appeared along my arm, my father knew then that I was more than just a mortal.

He didn't know I was mixed. I was only five. It scared the hell out of him." The tone of his voice dips and he studies the dark leaves at his feet. "He knew people would kill to get to me. They would use me like a weapon. I was never a child at all really." My heart sinks for him. Until I notice the traitorous feeling. I straighten my shoulders, pushing down the weak emotions. "So, he exhausted all of his resources for months until he found a way to get me to the mythical realm everyone whispers about." His eyes meet mine, intensity burning through them. "The Hopeless city."

A pounding feeling bangs through my chest, my heart racing from his words.

He could be lying. Everyone lies. These three could be no different.

But something in me believes every word he says.

Ryder just might be an exiled prince of Juvar. He might really have magic burning through his veins. He might really have saved my life tonight. The Hopeless city might be real after all.

But what he doesn't know is that I'll never step foot on the coast of that kingdom.

Chapter Four
The Eminence

The hike through the wooded area back to town is quiet. Not uncomfortably so. I enjoy the silence. I used to talk for hours to anyone who would listen. I used to talk about the most mundane things as if they held so much importance.

I was stupid then, taking for granted all the simple things in life that I'll never have again.

"My name's Daxdyn Riles." His name rolls off his tongue in a sensual way that makes me want to repeat it on an uneven and shuddering breath. I shake my head at my dirty thoughts just as he speaks again. "It's a nice sword." Daxdyn bumps his lean shoulder into mine.

I eye him for a moment, taking in his lithe muscle tone. The way a smile always sits waiting on his lips makes the suspicion in me fade away.

He isn't dangerous. I don't think he could be even if he tried.

My attention darts to his brother; the hulking opposite of the man at my side.

"It was my father's."

Why did I tell him that?

Stiffly, I straighten my posture as I chastise myself for speaking so freely with someone I know nothing about. I could know him though. Daxdyn could be useful if given the opportunity.

"Why didn't you just use your magic to escape the prison?" The tangle of trees ahead of us holds my attention. I try to pretend I'm not searching for information, as if I just want to make small talk.

The white moonlight falls across his smooth features. The iron-like color of his eyes shines with intensity. An odd thought crosses my mind, making me smile to myself: Daxdyn would make a beautiful prostitute. I push the smirk from my lips.

After my father's death, my aunt raised me. Lady Ivory is the most successful 'escort' in the country. She made sure I never was. But her words of wisdom have never left me. And I just know she'd encourage Daxdyn to use his good looks to his advantage.

And, oh, what an advantage he would have.

We would make beautiful fae babies, he and I.

"Iron depreciates fae magic."

"What?" I stutter out. It's hard but I pull my mind from the gutter to listen to what he's actually saying.

"Iron stunts it. The cell kept us locked up and it kept our magic safely locked away as well. A glimmer of it was all we could produce."

That is interesting. Maybe I should stop checking him out and listen a little more.

"Of course he would tell the pretty *human* all our secrets," Darrio says in a snide voice.

That's the second time he's used the word 'human' as if it's a slur.

With anger rising in me, my fist clenches at my side. The tightness of my jaw makes me want to scream. Then I want to hurl my small frame at his enormous back and beat my much smaller fists into his hard body. His hard, hard body.

Wait, what was I saying?

Ryder glances back to Daxdyn at the mention of magic. For a moment, I wonder if he'll tell him to shut up. A mortal shouldn't hear all their secrets. Even I think it's a shitty idea for him to be telling me this.

No one says a word though.

So, I pry even further.

"What if I asked you to prove you have magic?"

With confidence, I walk as if I'm not on the edge of my seat with hope that Daxdyn will show me an amazing magic trick. Something so great my mortal mind will be in awe of his ability.

Darrio turns to me, making me stumble from his abrupt stop. A feeling tingles between us from his nearness, making me lean into him subtly. It's like something inside him pulls at something within me. He appraises me slowly from head to toe, making me shift on my feet. A heated look is all he gives me before he quickly strikes his hand out and lightly touches his index finger to the tip of my nose.

A static sound accompanies his touch and a shock of pain strikes through the tip of my nose. Tingles spread all through my body, making me shudder.

My hand raises to my nose as I glare up at him.

Did he just boop my nose?

"That—" I pause as a smirk tilts the corner of my lips, "that was your amazing magic? That's it? Not very impressive."

Darrio cocks a brow at me and leans in ever so slightly closer to me. His breath fans across my jaw, taking away my sarcastic demeanor in an instant. "I'm a very controlling fae. If I wanted to burn you alive, I would have, human."

My breath catches from the thought of his threat and I can't decide if the word *controlling* is terrifying or arousing. When my ridiculous thoughts finally choose living over a simple orgasm, I push past him and continue walking next to Daxdyn. Daxdyn is the safer one, I can tell.

"Who captured you? How? How did someone capture three Hopeless?" They must be idiots. Too attractive for their own good. Too blind-sided by the beauty in life to see the danger all around them.

Daxdyn watches his boots as he walks. The leaves crunch beneath our steps and it seems to captivate his tense attention.

Silence fills the night. Nature speaks loudly while the four of us keep quiet.

I suppose revealing their one weakness is an

easier thing to admit than to say whatever it is Daxdyn is keeping from me.

"My mother." Ryder stares straight ahead, his steps coming more rapidly now. The sword at my hip brushes my thigh as I force my legs to keep up with their new pace.

A broken branch on the ground catches my normally cautious steps and I stumble. Daxdyn's warm hand wraps around my forearm. He holds the worn arm cuff on my forearm, his knuckles appearing whiter against the black fabric. A tingling calm spreads through me from his touch and I pull my arm from his reach.

"I'm sorry, what?" My feet stumble as I shift away from Daxdyn and race after Ryder and Darrio. They haven't slowed the slightest bit.

"My father fought so hard to keep me from the dangers of this world. I guess he didn't count on my step mother having different plans." Once again, he shoves his hands into his pockets. "When we entered this realm again last year, she drugged the three of us and demanded we give her what she asked for."

Why were they even in this realm?

"Why didn't you?" I ask instead.

"The Hopeless aren't gods; we're fae. Descendants of fallen angels. There are things outside of our abilities. Death, love, life. Ask all you want, but even the prophesized Eminence will have its limits."

Dread sinks through me, slowing my pace.

Ryder can't bring my father back. My lips purse as I glare hard at the ground.

"What's the Eminence?" I ask with a vacant sound filling my voice.

Ryder's wide shoulders become rigid. With a long hesitation, he turns his head to look back at me. His light eyes hold mine, weighing me down with just one look.

Right now, he's wondering if he can trust me.

He shouldn't.

I'm the mortal danger his father warned him about. I'm the big bad wolf, and he's all but begging me to guide him through the dark, dark woods.

If he screws up, I won't hesitate to kill him. This world is a game of life and I rather like my life.

Even if I am a homeless thief.

Looking up at him, it pains me to not appear vulnerable, to keep my natural features in place. My instincts tell me to appear as he wishes. It'd benefit me to be what he wants.

For some reason, I can't. Maybe it's because he saved my life. He pulled me back from the greedy claws of death. And now he's ruined me.

But it seems I've ruined him as well because he answers my question with nothing but honesty in his eyes.

"The Eminence is said to be the most powerful Hopeless in the entire world. Someday, the Eminence will come and it'll either rain wrath on this already demolished world, or it'll restore it to the beauty it once was."

A warm feeling spreads through me. Maybe the Eminence will restore it. I might one day breathe air that isn't tinged with smoke. I might bask in the warmth of sunlight. I might actually live a happy life.

Or the Eminence will destroy the world.

Well, you win some you lose some.

My thoughts fade and I feel something. I can physically feel the attention burning into me. My lashes flutter, and I look up to Daxdyn to find his eyes tracing across my features.

Pure confidence is all he possesses. Zero embarrassment is held within him for being caught checking me out.

A shiver skims down my spine as I narrow my hard gaze on his absurdly handsome face.

His tongue darts out and licks his lower lip before the smile falls into place there.

Gods above, this is going to be a long trip.

***

The coast is still at least a week's hike. It's been over a day and our pace has slowed to a near nonexistent speed.

"Let's camp here for a few hours. We'll start back up once we've had some decent food and some sleep." Ryder assesses the surroundings. A stream trickles along our path. It leads into town. I know it like the back of my hand. I also know we won't be robbed here. We're too far from the village for the lowlifes to find us.

Well, except for me, anyway.

"Daxdyn help me with the fish. Darrio can you get us a small fire going?" Both of the men nod to Ryder, mirroring one another like true twins.

Daxdyn and Ryder make their way down to the stream. I can almost hear the sound of their voices from several yards away.

Darrio turns from them and runs right into me, his chest brushes mine. My footing falters but I'm quick to right my steps. A scowl curls his full lips.

And yet, there's an energy swirling between us. I think it might be from the spark he rained down on my poor nose, but it's definitely … strange. It's like his body is charging mine, spiking energy all through it. My core tightens simply from the feel of his body against me.

"Fucking human."

What a delightful asshole this one is.

My jaw clenches at the word 'human'. He says it harshly. Like I'm beneath him and his kind.

What does this man have to be so unhappy about? I'm homeless and even I enjoy my life more than Darrio. A beat passes and we're still assessing one another.

A cruel, jagged line is slashed down his face. It isn't small; the imperfection demands attention. Without much thought, the smooth skin of the scar adorning his temple greets my fingertips.

He's so different from his twin it's almost astounding.

"You're not the same, are you? Not here." Not with every jagged imperfection that lines his scarred body. Not in the mind that's always turning. Not deep down inside.

Darrio doesn't flinch away from my touch. His eyes hold mine as I study the pink skin beneath my index finger. It runs the length of his dark hairline, from temple to jaw. What did Darrio do to deserve this? Oddly, it doesn't take away from his haunting good looks. It only magnifies it if anything. It highlights his light eyes. My gaze shifts to his depthless gaze. The scar draws attention to his always calculating and hard, glaring irises.

The energy I felt earlier is growing wild within my chest. My erratic heartbeat pounds restlessly.

His brows pull together in confusion. Does he feel it too? Or does my attention make him uncomfortable?

Good. He deserves to feel awkward for what he called me.

A smirk touches my lips and before I can speak again his mouth is on mine.

It's a reckless kiss. Flawed and rushed; our lips

angled against each other.

To my surprise, I lean into him with my arms held uneasily away from his hard body. Strong hands grasp my hips. Darrio holds me the way I used to hold the stolen trinkets I hid away as a child. His palms skim up my bare sides, against my ribs before meeting the cotton of my vest.

It's a kiss filled with fire and intent and all I want is for it to burn me up inside.

With a striking spark that tingles all through me, he parts my lips. Slowly he rolls his tongue across mine, sending that igniting feeling right through me. It's a feeling that wakes me up inside. A feeling that makes me snap.

I push back from him with more force than necessary. My palm connects swiftly with the scar along his jaw. The scar that got me into this mess in the first place. A sting explodes against my fingertips and a satisfying red mark tints his cheek.

The hateful words we've shared won't be forgotten with one kiss.

Even if it was a heart pounding, knee shaking, panty …

I shake my head adamantly. Not going to happen.

He looks to the ground. It's a confused look that almost makes guilt touch my stomach.

"I'm sorry." His throat bobs before he finally meets my eyes.

"You should be," to spite him I add, "*Rio*."

Thin lips pull across his features, his head shaking back and forth, rejecting the affectionate nickname just like I rejected him.

Light sparks, catching my attention. A blazing ember is held in Ryder's hand, lighting up his good looks in a golden hue. The fire rests in his hands as Daxdyn studies the stream they stand in. Daxdyn's shirt has been thrown to the ground and I couldn't tear my gaze away from his body if I wanted to. Even if his own brother is looking right at me.

"Fucking human," Darrio whispers once more before turning away from me.

His deep voice tingles across my skin.

A smile clings to my lips from his term of endearment. That's what I'll call his little name for me; endearing.

Another light appears, held tightly in Daxdyn's hands. He lowers his palms beneath the waters. Reflective colors ripple across the sharp angles of his jaw. Seconds pass with him standing ever so still. The muscles of his shoulders tense, and when he rises, he holds a large squirming trout in his hands.

It happens so quickly it's as if the fish was drawn to him.

He tosses the flopping fish to the grassy shore before resuming his stance and repeating the simple process.

I gape at them for so long I barely realize Darrio's somehow structured a blazing fire out of thin air. The crackle of logs burning pulls at my attention and I turn toward the warmth.

The last thing I want right now is to sit buddy-buddy at the campfire with Mr. Stick Up His Ass. I exhale slowly before taking a seat on the grass. Darrio doesn't even glance my way. He appears as if he's entranced with the flickering flames.

He doesn't seem to be the best at avoiding confrontation.

And neither am I.

The blazing hue makes his skin appear more bronze. The coloring washes away his scars but emphasizes the slight skew of his nose. It's as if it's been broken one too many times.

With movement so fast I barely see it, Darrio is at my side.

"Someone's coming. Get up. I can't let anything happen to you." He says it like I'm both a priority to him as well as an inconvenience.

He hauls me from the ground, gripping the underside of my arm with force as he drags me from our cozy spot.

I don't fight him. I don't argue or demand he let me go. I follow him without question.

It might even seem like I trust him.

For a second at least.

I jerk away from him once the thick woods seclude us. My eyes flicker to the river but it's empty. Daxdyn and Ryder are nowhere to be seen.

I'm still assessing our surroundings when he flings me against a tree. My teeth jar together. The bark bites into my spine and I glare up at him as he puts his finger to his lips. Lightly, his rigid body skims against mine as we both ignore one another to listen intently to …

Absolutely nothing.

"Is this your way of avoiding the awkward campfire silence?" I whisper in an accusing tone.

His head tilts slowly down as he glares at me like I'm the most ridiculous thing he's ever had the misfortune of protecting.

With one swift turn, he pushes away from me. At first, I think he's just sulking until he grips his hands around the large man's neck. The man's worn boots graze across the ground, frantic to be out of Darrio's strong grip. He lifts him a little higher, bringing the strangers face up to his own so he can closely appraise him.

"Who are you?" Darrio asks and his eyes hold an eerie, glinting look within them.

A choking sound gargles through the stranger's throat.

That seems to be Darrio's problem, though; he never puts his fists down long enough to let words pass.

"Release him and maybe you'll get a few answers."

Darrio's hard eyes land on me and he drops the man in an instant.

A warm feeling of triumph sinks into me. I'm actually stunned he listened to me at all.

A gasping sound leaves the man as he heaves

air into his lungs. Defiance shines in his dark eyes as he stares up at Darrio with a new, fearless look in his gaze.

"Who are you?" Darrio asks again. I, too, study the man as if I'm not completely distracted by the tone of Darrio's deep and demanding voice.

"I am the honored and loyal soldier of our lady, Queen Alexia of Juvar. I am one of many sent to retrieve you and your kind."

His endless title has me rolling my eyes on the spot.

Darrio kneels until he's right in the man's face again. A rapid tic has the fae's fingers arching toward his palm and a vicious light blazes through his fingertips.

A haunting look of aggression storms through Darrio's gray eyes. It's like hellfire is burning deep within him. His gaze isn't beautiful for once.

It's terrifying.

That look sinks realization into me. I now realize that I should not taunt this dangerous fae as much as I do.

A flickering image to my right startles me so much I gasp. Ryder stands staring down at Darrio and the solider, and Daxdyn holds Ryder's shoulder as if he needs the other fae to keep him in place.

An eerie feeling tingles through me as I look at them. Their bodies flicker in and out of focus as if they're not entirely there. As if they're not a solid form at all.

Ryder's fingers curl into a tight fist and then the two of them appear ... whole again. Daxdyn releases his shoulder and they both continue to look upon the man with disgust curling their lips.

"Tell your lady, the queen, that Darrio Riles is returning home." He brings his palm closer to the man's face, highlighting the apparent fear that clings to his features. His other hand sparks with magic, and he holds them both on either side of the soldier's jaw. "Tell her, I'll be greeting her with open arms."

Then Darrio slowly grips the man's face in his palms. A sizzling sound accompanies the screams of the most honored and loyal soldier of our lady, Queen Alexia of Juvar.

Chapter Five
Shuddering

For the last several miles nothing but open fields are all we've seen. The long strips of grass are rough against my palm as I pull at them. They tickle my skin with every step I take, flicking lightly against my abdomen and arms.

A comfortable silence has fallen over our little group. Since last night, I can't find it in me to pester the hell out of Darrio as I once did. He really can kill me without even trying if he wanted.

And I fucking stabbed him like he was nothing when we first met.

As we walk, my attention continues to dart over to his broad stature. Darrio Riles has the hard body of a warrior and the endless scars to match. He'd probably be handsome if he ever stops referring to me as *the fucking human*.

I shrug as I consider him.

My delightful attitude is seriously undervalued

with this one.

There's a town up ahead. The tiny houses are just shadowed forms against the starry night sky. The image of it alone makes me home sick.

The smell of smoke is harsher now, the closer to the coast we get. It'll be overwhelming when we get to the sea.

"What was that thing you did? When you and Daxdyn flashed in just in time to see that guy lose his face." I look to Ryder and he glances at me out of the corner of his pale blue eyes.

They decided to let Mr. No Face live. They said they wanted to make sure their message gets back to the queen.

A chill skims down my spine, but I straighten my shoulders and ignore it.

"It's called shuddering."

Fuck, that sounds perfectly named.

"It's like … teleporting for fae," he adds.

"Teleporting?" My brow arches and my feet stop walking all together. "You could have just flickered us right to the coast already without all this walking? I've had to look at Darrio's brooding face for days now."

Darrio scoffs at me but doesn't encourage my teasing.

"I can't shudder you."

A smile almost pulls at my lips at the phrasing of that sentence alone. The adult in me bites back my smirk even though I have no doubt in my mind that Ryder could shudder me real good.

"Why?" I study him closely.

He looks to the stars as if he's pleading with them to find reason within his little foolish human friend.

"You won't like the answer."

"Tell me," I demand.

Quiet laughter skims over Daxdyn's full lips and my eyes narrow on him.

"You're too heavy," Ryder finally says.

"Fuck you." My arms cross at the same time as my lips curl. "You're making excuses. You flickered Daxdyn, you can flicker me." Considering Daxdyn probably outweighs me by more than fifty pounds, it shouldn't be a problem.

"It's shuddering. Flickering isn't a thing." He pushes his hand roughly through his blonde hair.

"My fae power won't allow me to transport you. As a human, your energy is too heavy. You've never seen magic; your mind and energy is flawed by the black and white understanding of reality. Your energy is weighed down by the cosmics of reality."

Cosmics of reality.

This is the explanation I get for why we've been walking for days.

"Prove it."

"Prove it?" he repeats. His brows lower as he stares hard at me.

"Prove you can't shudder me."

Darrio's attention slowly drifts toward Ryder as he shifts on his feet. A long, drawn-out sigh leaves his lips; it's as if Darrio feels his precious time is being wasted.

Then the space between Ryder and I disappears as he shudders right in front of me. A daring smile clings to his lips as his image flickers slightly until he stands whole again. The ridges of his chest brush against my breasts and I can't think of a single snarky thing to say to him. All I can hear is my heart pounding a wild beat.

Without warning, he grabs my legs, lifting me up. His arm holds my back as he cradles my body against his. I let my palm trail up his chest, not meeting his eyes while I take my time praising the solid lines of his body to grip his shoulder.

His body is pure strength and power. I feel it held against me, but I feel it crackle around me as well. It's as if it's a tangible thing.

Fae magic.

Slowly his gaze drifts to my parted mouth and he rolls his tongue along his lower lip. I all but hum a pathetic moan of a response.

Then my breath catches as the world goes black. The nerves within my body snap against my flesh as if they're uncertain where they belong. It feels like my veins are trying to separate from my body. Pain shoots through me, like needles beneath my skin.

Then it stops. My eyes open to find us lying on the ground right where we were. Darrio glares down at me while Daxdyn offers up his hand.

I'm lying on top of Ryder, my hand splayed across his chest. My ass is on the hard ground, my legs thrown over his lap as if he might still try to carry me away. He's no longer holding me though.

With amusement, he leans back on his arms, making himself comfortable here in the dusty field.

"Happy?" he asks with an annoying cock of his brow.

My stomach sinks as I realize he wasn't lying. He can't shudder me.

"I feel like a fat ass, thanks."

He has the audacity to smirk that charming and exasperating little smile of his. I dust myself off and shove away from him. A groan slips from his lips even as he laughs at my poor attitude.

"I tried to tell you," he hollers after me, a smirk lacing his words.

My boots storm across the dry field and, without looking back, I flip him a gesture with one hand. The arrogant sound of roaring laughter is their only reply.

Assholes.

Chapter Six

Saint's Inn

The beautiful two-story home I grew up in possesses my attention the moment I step foot on the dusty streets in the middle of downtown. Divots line the path, making my steps uneven and jostled.

We've travelled together without further incident for two days now.

A dirty crowd of people, who are trading bread and fruit for blankets and clothes, stop their transactions the moment their beady little eyes land on the four of us.

A woman with creases along her withered features and deep brown eyes staggers nearer. Her hungry gaze watches us with too much interest. My shoulder bumps against Daxdyn's as I move closer to him. Darrio's heavy strides bring him between myself and the woman as Ryder walks close behind me, his steps almost brushing the back of my boots.

"The Hopeless," she whispers in a dry, crackling breath.

My gaze darts down to their arms. All three fae have their sleeves pulled down over the slashing marks of the Hopeless.

How does she know?

"May they return to us and save us all." Her hand rises as if she's seeing a powerful god, as if she can shine in our passing. As if these three men could save her tarnished soul.

They cannot save us from this broken world.

No one can.

A tenseness fills my jaw as I begin to walk faster, my head tipped down to the dusty roadway. With intent, I make my way to the one house in particular.

The house stands among a group of deteriorating homes. The others are missing chunks of walls. The boards covering their windows are old and warped, but the familiar homes protect the families inside them all the same.

The one I'm walking to isn't in shambles. It's as close to residential perfection this world will ever know.

The three men look to one another skeptically and their skepticism only rises when my knuckles rap against the polished wood of the house facetiously numbered 6969. The white brick is immaculately clean. The little golden numbers above the door glisten even in the pale morning sunlight.

With ease, the door glides open and a woman with long blonde hair sways into view.

"Kara, my little honey squeeze. I haven't seen you in nearly a year, my love." Her thin arms wrap intimately around me, holding me to her plump chest that's exposed over the tight corset of her silk gown. Her hand still drapes across my shoulders even after she pulls back from me. Her emerald eyes eat up every inch of the men behind me. "Who are your friends, Kara?"

I notice the way Daxdyn drags his gaze over my aunt, but the other two only offer kind smiles. Well, Ryder's smiling. Darrio's lips remain in a hard line across his stern face.

I haven't taunted Darrio once since I saw him burn the majority of a man's face off.

I've played nice.

Too nice.

"This is Daxdyn, Ryder, and Rio." Darrio pins me with a glare at the sound of my introduction and I applaud myself internally for getting under his skin with three simple letters. "Guys, this is my aunt, Lady Ivory."

Ryder's brows pull low at the formal title my aunt loves to be called. In all honesty, her name's Celeste. Celeste Storm. But Ivory Storm has a regal appeal. Full of beauty and prestige. Just like my aunt.

"Welcome to Saint's Inn, gentlemen." The purr in her voice hasn't changed a bit in the last few years. Nothing about her has changed. She's still as beautiful and kind as the day she took me in almost five years ago. "This is where the magic happens."

I scoff when the word magic falls from her lips. She has no idea who she's talking to with these three.

"Kara, can I have a word with you?" Ryder repeats my aunt's nickname for me and he takes the few steps up to her beautiful home. His chest pushes against my shoulder, his breath warm against my neck.

The excited gleam in my aunt's gaze shifts from Ryder to me and then back again.

I get the feeling sex is the only thing that ever fills her mind.

Part of me is irritated by her sex-filled life, and part of me is extremely jealous.

"Sure." I slip out of my aunt's embrace. I hate being touched, but somehow, it's different with her. It makes me feel like my father's still with me because I have her. I'd do anything for Ivory, and she'd do anything for me.

Lady Ivory watches us closely. She doesn't even pretend to ignore us. Ryder takes a few steps away, his hand gripping mine as he leads me back down the small stairs. My fingers twitch against his. The warmth of his rough palm against mine does something strange to me. Something unnatural. A tingling feeling stirs within me and I quickly pull my hand from his.

"What the hell are we doing here, Kara?" His tone is stern and makes me cringe from the sound of it. "We should not be hanging around outside, in the middle of a village. My step mother will find us. She already knows we've escaped. We need to lie low."

My arms fold across my chest. The cuffs along my forearms brush across my skin as I hold myself tightly.

"My aunt is the only family I have." Again, I hate that I'm telling them this. "I will not just skip past her house without stopping in. You have poor manners for a Prince of Juvar."

"*Former Prince*," he corrects and it almost makes me smile.

His rejection of the title does something weird to me. It makes me entirely too happy. It makes me … like him. I like him for not wanting something most people would beg to have; a title, a feeling of importance, power.

"Would the former Prince of Juvar care to come inside for some breakfast." My aunt places her hand on the curve of her hip and Daxdyn pushes past Ryder in an instant, their shoulders knocking slightly.

"Of course he would," Daxdyn says in a smooth voice.

My aunt's gaze ignites just looking at his beautiful face and I know exactly what she sees.

"You have the face," her fingertips skim his abdomen, "and body of a high value escort."

The easy demeanor he holds in his perfect posture fades just slightly as he seems to repeat her words in his head.

"Wh—what?" The ever-constant smile falls right off his face. It's replaced with a confused look that makes Darrio laugh out loud. His rumbling laughter causes me to smile and I glance at him. Darrio darts his gaze from mine, the happiness tearing from his features.

Daxdyn's pretty eyes are wide as he stares at my aunt with a new kind of awe in his gaze. Pushing past Ryder, I run to Daxdyn's rescue. My boots skip up the steps until I'm at his side.

"They're tired, Lady Ivory. Do not exhaust them further." Gods above, please do not offer them anything embarrassing. My new friends don't know this yet, but oral sex is considered a side dish here. They're in for an awakening if we linger in this house. "I'm going to shower. Please be nice to my friends."

"I'll only treat them how I know you should be treating them, Kara."

I cock an eyebrow at the serene smile resting on her beautiful face. A hint is laced through her careful words.

"Well, I'm an asshole to them. Please follow in my footsteps." A tight smile forms on my lips.

Her red nails skim up Daxdyn's bicep and his

brows pull together as he looks at her hand there. Something appears to be swirling in his mind, I can tell. He must be real close to an understanding.

"They deserve a bit more than that, don't you think?" my beautiful aunt pleads.

"No. No, they don't." I detach her palm from his arm and his mouth parts as he looks from me to her.

"Not even a teensie," she parts her index finger and thumb as her lips form a perfect pout, "little bit?"

"*Nothing.*" My brows arch high as I emphasize that she is not to offer them a single sexual thing. "Do not offer them anything. Please."

Why is it so hard to just not care? I shouldn't care. What do I care if one of them or all of them gets the house special?

My jaw clenches just thinking about it.

The men stare at us in confusion, clearly listening to our banter but not understanding any of it.

Her lips thin. Not a line creases her face. Lady Ivory looks more like my sister than my aunt.

"Fine," she says with a wave of her hand. "I'll

be a terrible host. Is that what you want to hear?"

Slowly, I nod to her.

The tension in my shoulders falls like I just won a strenuous battle instead of a plea for a sexless night. It feels strange trying to protect them. Even if it's only from my aunt's deviant behavior. I just want to keep them safe. From her. From sex ... with her.

What is wrong with me?

I roll my eyes at myself and begin climbing the glossy wooden stairs. A redhead in a tight corset and even tighter jeans passes me.

They'll know. The three of them will know what this place is the moment they're inside. I'll be enjoying a long, hot shower by then. I refuse to worry about them any longer.

"Kara," Lady Ivory's sweet voice calls up the stairs to me and my back stiffens all over again at the sound of my name. "I have a red dress in the closet. You'll like it. Stay for dinner, won't you?"

Dinner. Saint's Inn gets busy the moment the sun goes down. Staying for dinner would be ... entertaining and slightly awkward.

"I'll think about it."

I don't turn to her or say another word as my boots drag up the stairs. On the second floor, I pass two more beautiful women and they smile kindly at me. I don't have the strength to give them a kind look in return.

I push the door to my aunt's room open. High ceilings are cast in the white morning sunlight. The walls are a pretty shade of blue and are accented by stark white trim. A large four-poster bed, big enough for several people, sits in the center of the far wall.

She's remodeled since I've been here.

In our society, there are very few things that prosper any more. Technology was long ago replaced by magic. Then magic was ripped away. The bones of society are all that's left.

It's hard to even find food now. But sex will always be in demand.

Dirt crumbles from my boots as I cross her luxurious white carpet. My fingertips trail over the glossy dresser before opening the bathroom door. I close it behind me and turn the small lock in place. Locks are something of an obsession with me. If one is available, it will be turned. I'd lock the whole world out if I could.

It becomes too clear to me how badly I need a shower. My blonde tresses are dry at the ends; coarse between my dirty fingertips. Turning the silver knob, the shower clicks on. Lady Ivory's establishment is one of the few homes in town that has running water. This really is Saint's Inn.

White steam drifts through the room and I relish in the feel of it warm against my skin as I begin to undress. Lastly, I unwrap the black cuffs against my forearms.

When I first came to my father's sister for help, I had been alone on the streets for months already. I wore long gloves even then. She never asked, though I know she assumed they were to hide the self-inflicted pain I might be hiding. Those few months after he died were the hardest. I hated asking her for help. But she accepted me without question.

She's one of the few people who have accepted me in my life.

I push the thoughts from my mind as I slip beneath the scalding hot water. It rains down on me in relaxing patters across my shoulder blades. My eyes drift closed from the feel of it slipping across my skin. Water droplets cling to my lashes as I watch charcoal colored water spin down the drain at my feet.

I take my time here.

An hour passes and I don't give a damn. When I finish, I take my time combing through my pale locks. I apply my aunt's lotions generously to every inch of my skin. A scent of vanilla now clings to my body and I want nothing more than to take a long and lazy nap.

The soft carpet greets my steps as I make my way back into her room. I shiver from the cold air against my damp skin. Opening her closet, I see the dress in an instant.

Long, crimson fabric demands my attention.

Of course she was right. I do like it. There was a time I wore nothing but the best. Smooth silk gowns were all that ever touched my skin. I haven't worn a gown in years.

I pull the thin material from the hanger. The skirt is a single piece and the top is a much smaller piece. Yes, I like it very much.

The smooth dress skims up my thighs. I zip it up with ease and slip my arms into the top. It crosses over my shoulder blades and ties in a bow as if I'm a present to be opened. A two-inch sliver of my abdomen is exposed. The scar just below my ribs nearly peeks out.

Picking up my father's sword, I consider how the dirty blade will look against the soft dress.

Not very practical, I suppose.

I consider the other few weapons I possess. I'd hate to prance around without some sort of protection.

A gentle knock brushes lightly against the oak doorframe and I jump from the small sound.

Daxdyn looks up from the doorway. His messy hair threatens to spill into his gray eyes.

His lips part without sound as his gaze burns across every inch of my body.

"Wow. You look..." Again his lips part without the assistance of words.

"Decent?" I ask with a smile.

The handsome smirk he always has fills his face. Dimples crease his cheeks making my knees go weak at the sight of them.

"Well, you're no high dollar escort but, yeah, you look decent."

I bite my lip to stop the smile from growing on my face. My feet are still bare and I cross the room to where he stands.

"Did you need something, Daxdyn?" If I'm being honest, the words are intentional. I can practically see the dirty thoughts slamming through his mind.

He tilts his head down to admire me closer. He towers over me without my shoes and I find myself wanting to lean into his hard chest.

He's not built like the other two. He's more lithe instead of bulky. He's not skinny or wiry. The muscle tone is cut solid. It lines his body, as if he's never eaten a single carb in his entire life.

"Your aunt said it'd be a good idea if I went and checked on you."

I cock my brow at him. She's ridiculous. She sent him up here with all her hopes and dreams that we'd be having sex by now.

She probably made a small sacrifice to the gods in the name of my orgasm.

Lady Ivory is that little devil some people have that whispers terrible ideas into their ear at the worst possible time.

She's going to get him into trouble.

Does Daxdyn know that?

"This place is a whore house, isn't it?"

His blunt words cause a bubble of laughter to part my lips. I swallow down the sound and nod. My eyes drift to his dusty black boots.

"You don't have to be embarrassed about it, Zakara." Carefully, he leans into the white doorframe, coming slightly closer to me.

"I'm not embarrassed. I'm never embarrassed." Skepticism lines his brows as if he knows me better than I do. "She's the only family I have and she's the most successful woman I've ever met."

"You should be proud. In this world, most women die without the protection of a man." His fingers skim the inside of my wrist just lightly and I shift away from him and his affectionate touch. "You and your aunt are strong. Never be embarrassed by that."

He leans into me even further and my spine stiffens from his closeness. He doesn't reach out to me as he presses a kiss to my temple. Warmth sears through me from the small contact.

It's then that I know he's the one that held me close when I thought I was dying. A shiver races through my entire body.

Without another word, he brushes past me and heads toward the bathroom.

The door clicks shut behind him and I realize how loud my heart sounds in my ears.

Then I feel someone's attention on me and I look up in time to see Darrio standing on the top step, staring at me with steely eyes.

"You kissed him too, huh?" His voice is all deep rumbles and sneering laughter.

My brows lower as I wrap my arms around myself. The dress no longer feels pretty. It feels weak. Exposing. Fragile.

"I didn't kiss him, you demented asshole." My eyes narrow on him and he takes his time walking closer to me. His boots scuff across the shining hardwood floors of the hallway. Rage flies through me as a taunting smile touches his lips. His amusement only urges me on. "For the record though, when I *do* kiss him, I won't push away from him. His touch won't repulse me. I won't flinch away from your brother, Darrio. I promise you I'll enjoy it." Every clipped word is spoken with vengeance. The shitty words he's said to me since the moment we met are fueling my terrible anger.

He looks down on me. His wide shoulders fill the span of the doorway but I don't shrink back from him.

"You really think you're the first woman to reject me for my brother?" A low, gravelly sound fills his voice. It's the same tone I thought was so sexy the first time he spoke. His head dips low until he's right in my face. "You think you're so fucking special, human? You're not. You're nothing." Only an inch separates his lips from mine as he breathes out the last part on a whisper. "Just like me."

My lower lip trembles as I stare up into his hard eyes. My own furious reflection is all that I see in his gaze. Our bodies are nearly touching; sparking with the anger fuming between us.

This reaction always floods through my body when it comes to him. This tingling fury that sets me on edge just because he's near.

"I *am* nothing, Rio. But someday I'll be happy. I'll be loved. And you'll still be alone. Alone and an asshole."

My heart claws at my chest, demanding I push him even further.

Reaching back, I grip the handle and slam the door in his face. I feel it bang into his head as it closes with a jarring sound.

The groan he emits from the other side of the

door causes my lips to pull up in a small, satisfied smile.

Darrio is a cruel man, but he's not the worst I've ever met. He'll have to dig a little deeper if he expects to get a real fight out of me.

With burning rage, I pull on soft gloves. They're extravagant and caress my upper arms. They make me feel better.

The expensive material reminds me of a time when I wasn't just nothing. When I had hopes and dreams and a life worth living.

When I was more than just a thief.

Chapter Seven

Beautiful Harmony

Not once do I think of the things Darrio said to me. For the remainder of the day I laugh with my aunt. We reminisce about the days when I lived here. As if we were a normal, happy family.

We were never normal. But we were happy.

She and I stand on the porch alone. The wind pulls at my hair, causing it to flick across my lips. The sun burns wildly across the horizon, threatening to darken our already dark world. It almost looks untouched here. The destruction isn't as bad here as it is in Juvar.

The aftertaste of the ash in the wind is the only hint that something is amiss.

"Do you think you'll settle with one of them?" She glances into the house at them.

The fact that she used the word settle makes me

want to laugh. No woman on the planet will ever consider it 'settling' if they come across any one of them.

They each have their flaws, no worse than I do, but they're … what every girl hopes for, really.

Confidence and intelligence. Sexiness and wit. Loyalty and strength.

If only the three of them could somehow form one perfect man.

And maybe that man just doesn't speak. Maybe he just hangs out as this intelligent, sexy—slightly aggressive—loyal man. Who. Does. Not. Say. A. Damn. Word.

Two of the three men are shoveling food into their mouths and smiling. Darrio hasn't touched a bit of his food. I wonder if he feels guilty.

I doubt it. I doubt he's ever felt guilt in his entire life.

"The three of them are just looking for a guide. I'm only helping them."

"Why? I've never known you to do anything out of the kindness of your little black heart, Kara."

I roll my eyes at her, making a smile tilt her full lips.

"Who would you choose, if you had the chance?" I ask her. A wicked smile pulls at my features. It's a dirty thing to ask. It's something that sends a thrilling feeling spiraling through me.

She touches her finger to the center of her mouth as if she's really having a hard time deciding.

"I wouldn't."

"You're lying." My words are so high it draws the attention of all three men. They look my way and my cheeks flame from the conversation that's being spoken about them. I'm asking her to pick one as if they're livestock, and she's saying she wouldn't. What a terrible liar she is.

She leans into me, the smirk still kissing her lips. "I wouldn't," she repeats in a whisper. "Choose, that is. Why choose? Those three care about you. Let them care about you, Kara. All. Three. Of. Them. I'd never have to worry about you again if you had three protectors."

"You know the real world works slightly different from life within Saint's Inn, right? In real life, I can't just screw around with three men. It would end very badly."

"For the wrong people, yes, it would end in

disaster. But for the right ones it could end in harmony." Her attention pulls back to the three of them who are still watching us intently. "Beautiful harmony."

She sounds so full of knowledge. Dangerous and sexy knowledge.

"Well, this isn't about *grinding harmony*."

"I said nothing about grinding. Push the dirty thoughts from your head." Her white teeth sink into her lower lip before she becomes serious once more. "What is it about? What do you get out of it?"

The pink and purple shades of the sky hold my attention as I carefully ignore her invasive question.

I don't even know what I get out of it any more. They can't change the fact that my father's dead …

She only lets a beat pass before carrying on to the next topic.

"Do you remember Mackel?"

A warm feeling spreads through me at the mention of his name.

Mackel Alexander was my first kiss. And Gods

above, could that boy kiss.

"Yeah, I think so," I say as vaguely as possible.

"You're a dirty liar, Zakara Storm." Her smile lights up her emerald eyes and I can't help but laugh. "He's our liquor supplier. Alcohol has made him very successful. He asked about you."

"When?" I hate how quickly that reply came.

"When he dropped off our order this afternoon. He saw you and asked about you."

Suspicion claws through me. Her words are carefully aimed. I can feel something coming. Something she's already put into place.

"What did you say to him?"

"I said he could ask for himself. Tonight. When he picks you up."

My nails bite into my palm as I fist my hand tightly.

"I cannot go on a date tonight. There are three men waiting for me. I can't just prance around as if they aren't important."

"*Are* they important to you?" Her pale blonde brow arches as high as it'll go as she looks down at me. I feel like she's the adult once more and I'm just the small child complaining about the chores she's asking me to do.

Not that the three of them are chores … or that I'd *do* them …

"Perhaps you should let the three men see you with another to make them see your value. If they have no interest in a beautiful woman, I promise you someone else will." A pleased smile rests on her lips.

As if mechanically, my eyes roll at her. She was always doing this. Always looking for a good man to steal me away from this corrupted fairytale my life somehow turned into.

But I don't need a man.

I have me.

"I'm not going—"

"Zaraka Storm." His smooth, deep voice vibrates through my every pore. It's the most masculine sound I've ever heard.

Yeah. Eat shit, Darrio. Your sexy voice has been replaced.

At the bottom of the steps stands a familiar man. The smile on his face is so perfect I have a hard time looking away to admire the rest of him.

Golden, depthless eyes shine with kindness. Broad shoulders hold his posture ever so straight. Hard muscles chisel down into lean hips.

"I guess I filled out a little since we were kids, huh?" His words try to pull my appreciation away from his strong body and it takes everything in me to deter my gaze. Again, my attention lands on that gorgeous smile.

Slowly he climbs the few steps until he's just in front of me.

"Looks like you've filled out too." His full lips have me in a trance.

I should speak, or at least close my mouth.

Nothing. I have no intelligent thoughts.

"You look very beautiful tonight, Kara." He leans into me, stealing up some of the terrible space that separates his body from mine.

"Thank you, Mackel." It comes out as a whisper. An astounded whisper. He was once a boy who kissed me like a man. Now he stands before me as nothing but masculine confidence.

Boots skimming over hard wood floors echo through the house behind me and I suddenly realize we have an audience.

"Who's your friend?" Ryder's calm voice carries over the rushed whispers of Daxdyn and Darrio.

I turn to the three men who are staring daggers at Mackel. He gives them a simple, polite smile.

They're more than I bargained for. When I stand on the shore and demand my reward for this journey, nothing but all the wealth in the world will be enough.

I swivel my gaze back to the tall, dark, and handsome man before me.

"Ready?" I ask, my smile as charming and beautiful as ever.

His large hand clasps mine. Not another word is spoken as he guides me away. To where, I'm not even sure.

"Fucking human." I hear Darrio's slur from several feet away and Mackel glances down on me with a look of confusion.

"He's weird. Don't worry about him." I wrap my hand around his bulging bicep and even bat my lashes up at him as a perfect smile kisses my lips.

It's then that I realize the amount of effort I'm putting into just being around Mackel. I hadn't even noticed it, but the last few days have been easy. Nothing I've done has been premeditated.

A sick feeling twirls within me at the realization of how dangerous it is to trust these strangers. I don't even know them and yet here I am.

I've been entirely myself with the three of them. My stomach sinks low. I've been *too* comfortable with them.

Starting tonight, that'll change.

Chapter Eight

Prince Charming

Tonight was simple. It was almost fun even. Mackel took me to his bar. The lights there were dim and just oozed expensive vibes. Naturally, I stole every single thing my fingers touched.

It was truly a wonderful evening.

The two of us stand on the small front porch of house 6969. A few wooden chairs sit to the left and I wonder if he'll linger; if he'll take a seat to talk for a while. I'm tired. Tired of pretending everything he says makes my heart melt. He's nice. Just as nice as he was when we were sixteen. But nice never made my heart demand someone's presence.

Hell, at the very least, even Darrio has an alluring appeal. I want to know where every scar on his body came from. I also don't want him to open his mouth to tell me. If he opens his mouth, only awful words will come out, I just know it.

"What are you thinking about?" Mackel asks as his hard body leans into mine. Every inch of him aligns in a suffocating way against me.

My cheeks flame red as I realize I was somehow thinking about Darrio of all people.

"You, of course." At the sound of my quiet words, that beautiful smile pulls at his full lips. "Just you," I whisper as his lips meet mine.

The warmth of his hands seep into me as he cradles my head. Expertly, his tongue drifts over mine. My back is flat against the house, pinned in place by his strong chest.

Slowly, my fingers run down his soft shirt. The lines of his muscles threaten to deter me from my real mission.

With purpose, I moan into his mouth. His breath quickens just as my fingers wrap around the pocket watch. It's taunted me all night with the gleaming gold chain hanging from his hip.

Warm hands drag down my chest, down my bare ribs, and across my hip to finally stop at the high slit in my tight dress. He pushes at the smooth material, searing heat into my flesh as my thighs lock together instinctively.

If he paws all over me too much he'll find an

embarrassing wade of cash pressing against my cleavage and there's nothing less attractive than stolen dollars slipping from your boobs.

I pull back from him, my eyes anxiously shining up into his.

"I like you." The words are a forced confession but they don't make his hand fall from its place high on my upper thigh. The scruff of his strong jaw meets my lips as I kiss his cheek delicately. "Pick me up again tomorrow night. I'll have a surprise for you." Another kiss skims his jaw with the tease of my promise.

It's a lie.

I'll be long gone tomorrow. Probably just as he realizes how much money he's missing out of the cash drawer.

"But tonight isn't over." That charming smile slashes across his face before twisting into something dangerous as he smashes his lips to mine.

A pounding sound thrashes through my chest. My fingers splay against his shoulders but his enormous body doesn't budge an inch beneath my shoving palms.

"Stop," I grind out between forcefully clenched

teeth.

The pressure of his lips against mine intensifies, bruising my lips as his warm hand slips beneath the high slit in my dress.

A mixture of anxiety and anger floods me.

Sharp teeth sink into his lip. There's nothing sexy about it. I bite hard enough for his warm blood to fill my mouth and he jerks back from me. Rage as hot as fire burns in his eyes. His glare pierces into me as his palm snaps across my cheek.

Stinging pain shoots through my jaw, making me flinch but I don't cry out. His hands grip my wrists. The hard wall meets my spine as he slams me back into place beneath his powerful body.

Then his body is spiraling away from mine. Boots thunder across the shaking porch. Ryder's shoulders are strung tight with power. He gives Mackel a violent shove. The man's feet stumble down the steps and he lands hard in the dirt.

Ryder's fists shake as if something within them demands to be released.

Mackel's jaw shudders before he snaps it shut. Blood stains his lower lip. His golden eyes dart from me to the man between us. My back is still against the wall, my palms pressed there as well, to keep them from shaking. I've felt worse fear before. Right now, anger trembles through me in waves.

Mackel isn't nearly as nice as I thought he was.

Ryder folds his arms across his chest, making him appear even bigger than normal.

As he stands, Mackel spits. A crimson color tinges his saliva. With a careless swipe of his thumb, he wipes the blood from his chin.

"If you were already busy tonight," his attention falls to Ryder, "all you had to do was say so, Kara."

Slowly he shakes his head back and forth. It's like I can see his mind working. He considers Ryder one more time, his eyes flickering back to me before he apparently declares me a waste of his time. He turns his back on us and strides down the road.

"Good night, Mackel." The whisper of my voice quivers and I blink hard.

Why do I do this to myself? My heart stings as I wonder if my father would be embarrassed by the situations I put myself in to survive.

Ryder finally turns toward me, and an angry

line is pulled between his brows.

"I didn't need your help. Not everyone is as defenseless as they appear." I stand to my fullest height and let my hands rest high on my hips.

With deliberate slowness, his gaze travels down my body, taking in the way the thin material of my dress hugs my hips, the way my shirt doesn't touch my skirt and leaves my slim abdomen exposed to the cool night air. He seems to linger on the top of my breasts that are carefully pushed up for maximum approval.

He slouches down into the closest chair, his shoulders hanging low. A look of exhaustion pulls at his blue eyes.

"What did you expect to happen on this date tonight with you dressed like that?" Glaring anger stings his voice.

"I thought I would come out ahead."

I flick open my palm and the gold chain swings with vengeance as I release Mackel's pocket watch for Ryder to admire.

For a second he only stares at the pretty talisman.

"How did you even get that?"

"Gotta be good at your job." I cock my head at him, my long hair shifting with my every move. The tight red dress shifts with my body, like water clinging to my skin.

I know what I look like. And I know how to use my body. It's my greatest weapon and my biggest torment. If I could be plain, average, and overlooked, perhaps my life would be different. But it isn't and I am not.

"Not everyone is distracted by a pretty face." His eyes narrow on me, igniting me with his attention. It's like he's daring me; pushing me to admit I was wrong.

To prove a point, I lift my leg and slip it over his lap, tilting into him as I settle onto his lean hips. At the feel of my body against his, he closes the small space that separates us. Without hesitating, his hands push up the smooth material of my dress, his palms skimming hot against my outer thighs. A shiver slips across my flesh. My fingertips run up his broad chest.

It's different with him and I. I don't know what it is, but I'm not a persona planning out her next haul with him. I can't think straight when Ryder's around. I couldn't carefully plan my words for him even if I tried.

His heated gaze drops to my lips.

"Have you ever stolen from me, Zakara?"

The three of them were prisoners. I realized they had nothing to steal within the first minute of meeting them.

From beneath my lashes, I meet his gaze. Our mouths are so close I can taste his breath against my tongue.

"Do you have something worth stealing, my Prince?"

His head dips low. The wild pounding of his heart can be felt against my palm.

Faintly, his lips brush mine. My eyes flutter as a tingling feeling spirals through me. Then he stops, his eyes widening with alarm.

"I have a girlfriend." The warmth of his fingers against my body slips away as he holds his hands out at his sides, as if he wants the gods to smite him down.

Right now, I kind of do too.

Neither of us move, though. I keep my hands planted against his chest as I stare into his captivating eyes. My mouth is just a breath away from his. His cruel mouth that said the worst possible thing at the worst possible time.

"Of course you do," I finally say, my eyes fluttering closed before I shove hard against his shoulders and stand. My thighs clench together, remembering the way it felt to be pressed against him. "Next time," my lips purse as I stare down at him, "do not interrupt my date."

"You want me to let you get yourself into trouble? To get yourself hurt?"

My hands press high on my hips. A twisting smirk pulls at my lips and the mere sight of it causes confusion to cross his handsome face.

Ryder's too handsome for his own good. Too charming. Too much of a prince for me to ever really care about him.

"I can take care of myself."

His blonde brow arches high.

Slowly, I push my palm seductively down my own torso, my smooth skin kisses my fingertips. Ryder's rapt attention takes in my every move. The soft, lavish material greets my palm as I skim down to the high slit against my thigh. His tongue licks against his lips as he watches me with a mixture of confusion and daring appreciation. My hand sneaks beneath my dress ever so slowly. With a quick flick of my wrist I pull the dagger from the holster between my legs.

The disgusted curling of his lips and the thin line between his brows almost makes me laugh out loud.

"Where the hell were you hiding that thing?"

The look on his face seems like I just revealed a detachable dick instead of a small knife.

He looks down my thin frame, his attention zeroed in on my thighs and the curve of my hips. The thighs and hips that were just pressed against him.

"I have many talents. Like slicing an assailant's dick off without lifting a finger."

I roll the blade in my hand, the dim lighting streaking across the glittering shine of it. Ryder's strong legs shift awkwardly and he puts his hand over his crotch.

"Fucking be careful next time."

"Next time I what?" I take a step closer to him, leaning down until I'm eye level. "You don't have to worry. I'll never be that close to your dick ever again." My skirt drifts across his dirty boots as I saunter past him without looking back.

It's then that I see how terrible the four of us are together. One of us might kill the other before we ever reach our destination.

Chapter Nine
The Middle

Soft moans drift through the house like a mortifying, orgasmic ghost haunting my thoughts.

"Stay the night," my aunt pleads. "I worry about you, especially at night. Leave in the morning." She holds out two keys in her palm for us.

She's trying to get me to stay; not just for the night, but forever. I could never stay here. I left for a reason. Deep down inside I'm terrified of staying here. I know if I stay I'd be too proud to find a man to depend on. I'd try to make my own way in life. I'd turn out just like Ivory. She's a role model to me. The only one I have really. But she has no idea what love is. In her mind, sex and love are one and the same.

Though I'll never admit it, I want love. I want the fairytale.

I want more from life.

I shake my head at her just as Ryder takes the keys from her hand.

"Thanks. I think we all need some sleep." He doesn't look at me. He hasn't once since our little episode on the porch.

A beaming smile is all she gives me as I pass.

"It's the last two doors on the right. *Goodnight*, Kara." Her words have a hint of amusement in them that have me doubting every step I take.

The sounds of pleasure vibrate though the walls, sending a nervous energy clawing through me. Ryder holds out his hand and Darrio scoops up one of the small silver keys. He makes his way to the top of the stairs first and goes to the last door on the right. The key slides in with ease and he swings it open quickly.

The three of us are just behind Darrio when he walks inside and shuts the door behind him with a deliberate clicking sound.

A locking sound.

"Guess it's just the three of us." Daxdyn winks at me, and I repay the playful look with a glare that makes the smirk on his face quickly disappear.

My clothes sit on a small table between the two

bedrooms. They're neatly folded and appear to be freshly washed.

Ryder opens our door as I gather up my clothes. We walk inside to find the real meaning behind my aunts taunting words.

One. Fucking. Bed.

There's only one bed set delicately against the far wall.

"I call 'not it' for middle," Ryder says so quickly I barely grasp the meaning.

"What?" Then it hits me.

"Not it," Daxdyn and I both chime at once.

We stare at one another in a childish stand-off.

"Why would I sleep in the middle?" He smirks down at me. His smile makes my stomach knot peculiarly. But, in this moment, I also want to rip that smile right off his sneering face.

"And why the hell would I take the middle?"

"Well," he says as if he's prepared to make an epic presentation of an argument.

He tilts his head back and forth his hands gesturing from Ryder to himself to me. He doesn't say a word as if I'll just fill in the blanks with his ridiculous game of charades.

"Because I'm a girl?"

"Exactly."

"No."

"No?" he repeats as if it's a question.

"That is an invalid argument. I'm going to need you to do better."

He looks to the ceiling as if he's really trying.

"I'll rock, paper, scissors you for it." His eyes hold mischief in them as if he's already won. As if I'm already pressed between the two beautiful men.

Ryder stands near the bathroom, his arms folded across his wide chest as he watches the two of us squabble over the middle.

"Fine."

"Or, if you wanted, you could always go ask Darrio to share his bed."

I would bet my life that there's only one bed in that room as well. And that bed would be even smaller with Darrio and his overbearing anger.

"I'll take my chances here."

His smile flashes larger. "I think you two are too much alike."

The words crash into me hard.

I'm nothing like Darrio.

"Stop stalling," I say sharply.

Sitting my clothes down in a chair, we step a little closer to one another and hold our fists over our other palm. Our fists shake once, twice, three times and ...

"Scissors beats paper." I hold my mock scissors up for him to see that I've won.

"How the hell did she beat you?" Ryder asks from his place a few feet away.

My brows pull together. Daxdyn's mouth falls open as he stares at me as if I've just done a form of black magic his fae people have never seen before.

"I'm going to change and when I come out please make sure my side of the bed is spacious enough for me." I all but stick my tongue out at Daxdyn before sauntering away.

The door clicks closed behind me and I twist

the silver lock into place. Their whispers filter into the small bathroom as I push the heavy dress from my body and step back into my worn jeans and vest.

The bathroom is a gleaming white color with dim lighting. I take my time washing my face and hands as I listen to them for a few moments.

"Did you let her win?" Ryder asks in a hushed tone.

He truly sounds astounded that I won the simple game.

"Why would I let her win? You think I want to be pressed against your dick all night?" A smirk touches my lips at the image he's painting. "I don't know. I guess I just wasn't focusing well enough."

"She distracting you?"

"What? No." Daxdyn's dismissal nearly makes me scoff as I lean into the smooth hardwood door.

"Good. We don't need any distractions. She's just our guide. We need her. Don't screw it up." And on and on Ryder's lecture goes until I finally swing open the door.

Their words halt the moment I walk through the room. They've stripped down to their boxers but I don't give them a second glance as I slip beneath the cool covers.

The lights flicker off and I feel the mattress dip as one of them climbs into bed. I face the window, watching the white light of the full moon filter into the dark room. Daxdyn's leg brushes mine as he settles in at my side. Another jostling of the bed tells me Ryder has also joined us.

A smile touches my lips. Never in my life did I think I'd be sharing a bed with two beautiful fae. I guess if I did imagine it, it'd be a little more … dirty? Yes, definitely dirtier.

The bed is the softest thing I've slept on in years. It welcomes me, pulls me into it and demands that I sleep soundly.

Moments pass, my eyes closing heavily. The sound of light, content snores fill the room. I'm going to sleep well tonight, I can feel it.

"Trade me places."

My jaw clenches at the sound of the harsh whisper. My eyes peel slowly open.

Daxdyn is one of those men who are referred to as 'man-child', I'm sure of it.

"Go to sleep, Daxdyn." The whisper is clipped.

Closed argument.

He squirms against me, his hard body skimming against my soft curves.

"Ryder's breath keeps brushing my neck. How am I supposed to sleep like this?"

A smile tilts my lips and finally I roll until we're face to face.

A subtle hint of a point tips the tops of his ears and I wonder if they all hold that small, telling trait.

It's unfair how attractive Daxdyn is. The white light kisses his already pale chest, making him appear porcelain and perfect. His smooth features might never age for all I know.

I physically want to give him everything his shallow heart desires. But I shove that feeling down.

"Just imagine what will be brushing against you tomorrow morning." I say the words slowly and carefully to him.

Silence passes between us before his eyes widen with horror. I wonder if he's imagining Ryder's erection with as much detail as I am.

"Trade me places, please, Kara." Secretly I

love the way he says my name. The hard 'k' sound is followed by a breathy tone that makes my thighs clench together.

I bat my lashes as I pretend to consider his plea. Several seconds pass during my *consideration*.

"No."

He bites his lower lip slowly and my attention falls to his mouth.

Daxdyn is good at playing with his looks to get his way. But what he says next isn't a game at all.

"I'm not one for blackmail, but I just want you to know," his gray eyes bore into me, "I didn't tell the others." The seriousness that fills his face sinks into me. Weighing me down with dread.

"Tell them what?"

"That I felt the mark of the Hopeless on the inside of your wrist today." His steady words take aim, and they obliterate the terrified pounding of my heart into sinking pieces that now lay heavily in the bottom of my stomach.

"I wasn't sure until I tried to press my way into your mind to win our little game. I couldn't do it. If you really were a simple human, I could have forced my way in to see all your hopes and desires." I'm breathing hard and I can't think of a thing to say to get out of this. "Why are you hiding it? You could have told us of all people."

My knee's pull up to my chest and my arms wrap around them instinctively. The memories of my father's death drill through my mind.

"He died." My voice cracks and I swallow the weak sound down before I speak again. "My father died in the city of Juvar. My markings didn't come until I was sixteen. The markings came during the king's funeral." My voice lowers even more as I speak about the king that I know is Ryder's father. "Everyone in the kingdom came. For miles and miles, people grieved their one true king. The markings slashed into my body so hard I fell to my knees with pain. I fell right in front of the queen. She was the first to see them and she demanded I be detained."

The feelings tumble through my chest, building there until I can barely breath. Fae are rare in this world, nonexistent really, and the Hopeless are all but a myth now. His step mother wasn't about to lose a possible fae.

"My father fought the soldiers off the best he could and I ran. I should have helped him." The tiny sound of my voice makes me sick.

"Nothing good would have come of you fighting them. They would have locked you away just like they did us."

"She killed him." I clench my eyes tightly closed as the image of her knife sinking into his stomach fills my mind. "She killed him because of me."

A warm hand skims up my arm. Daxdyn brushes his palm back and forth against my flesh. A tingling feeling pushes into me. It's an unnatural feeling that makes me want to sink into him and let him surround me.

"Is that your magic?"

My damp eyes open to him and he nods.

"I'm better at emotions than the others. Every fae is different. I hold the power of empathy. I can feel and manipulate emotions."

"Isn't that awful? Feeling everyone's emotions?"

"When someone's sad, it's a crushing feeling. It jars through me with more energy than I'm ready for. Most of the time, I don't truly have emotions of my own." Pity sinks low into my stomach from his words. "But occasionally," his finger trails down my arm, sending a shiver right through me, "occasionally their emotions sync up with mine. It's a euphoric feeling. A sensuous feeling."

A swirling energy begins to flutter at my core.

"And Darrio?"

His eyes close slowly as if it pains him to even think about it.

"Don't even get me started on Darrio. Rage and magic aren't a good mix. He's a fire fae, mostly. He isn't a bad guy." A pointed look is all I give him. "He's just ... an unintentional asshole."

Laughter shakes through me.

An unintentional asshole.

How fitting.

I smile at him and his warm palm skims up my shoulder until his hand is pushing the long blonde strands of hair back from my face. A different feeling begins to sink into my heart and I wonder if it's my own feeling or if it's something Daxdyn is gifting to me.

"Come to the Hopeless realm with us, Kara. It's right by Juvar." His whispered plea makes my knee's knock together.

He's wrong, though. The marking isn't the

same. Similar, but not the same. I've studied the markings on my arms for years. They aren't the same as the mark of the Hopeless.

The mark of the Hopeless is several black, angled lines pointing like an arrow to the wrist.

Mine's ... different. I'm not fae. I'm just scarred.

The only power I hold is my ability to survive. And to piss Darrio Riles off without even trying.

Long ago, this little town, New Haven, was named after its ports along the coast. 'Haven' for harbor. But there's more to it than that, I can feel it. It truly is a haven for me. There's a safety this village brings me, the likes of which I never felt on the island of Juvar.

My stomach sinks low. I can never return to Juvar. Therefore, I'll never find the Hopeless realm, even if I am fae like he says.

"Trade me places already," I tell him, changing the subject swiftly.

For a moment, he only studies me before slowly nodding. His light eyes hold something in them. Something burning. It's as if he's dying to say more but he won't.

The blankets shift as he lifts himself. He turns until he's above me, his strong arms caging me in beneath his lithe body. I roll to my back, ready to scoot to the dreaded middle.

Ever so slowly he licks his lips as he lowers his hips between mine. The spark in his eyes captivates me, stealing my breath away as my heart quickens its pace.

I like the way he feels against me. I like the way he's looking at me. And if I'm being honest, I like Daxdyn.

But, as Ryder said, I'm just their guide. If he was smart, he'd listen to Ryder. If he was smart, he'd run far, far away from me. Nothing good ever follows me, and nothing good could come from our friendship.

His hips settle more, a slow shifting of his body against mine. My eyes close as my lips part. Hard muscle presses against the curve of my breasts as I push myself up. His jaw skims my lips and, ever so quietly, I whisper against his neck, snapping his hopes in half with my words.

"That's not going to happen, Daxdyn," I force myself to say.

He breathes out a laugh and he lowers himself,

dragging his hard body against me. Gently he places a kiss to my forehead and my eyes close. Then he's pulling back and, before I know it, he's resting at my side.

And just like I said I wouldn't be, I'm pressed comfortably between the two beautiful fae.

Chapter Ten

A Good Day

Morning comes too soon. I feel burdened and free all at once. Strong arms are wrapped around me. It isn't until my eyes flutter open that I realize they're both Daxdyn's and Ryder's.

My head lies in the crook of Daxdyn's arm and his hand is tangled into my hair. His other hand rests on my arm, holding me to his smooth chest. Another hand is slipped across my side from behind and it's pressed flat against my lower abdomen.

A tingling feeling spreads all through me, settling restlessly in my stomach.

And where are my hands?

One is held against my own chest. That one's the good one; the well-behaved one. The other traitorous and wandering hand lies half beneath the band of Daxdyn's boxers and half out.

The fingertips of my left hand are dangerously close to the hard bulge straining against the black material of his underwear.

Heat pools between my legs as I consider skimming my index finger along his length. The covers shift behind me and I realize Thing One isn't the only cock I'm entirely too close to.

Thing Two snuggles into me and the moment he moves the shifting begins. His hips are pressed so tightly against my lower back my legs actually shake.

I can't really be judging Thing One and Thing Two though. My own hips are pressed against Daxdyn's side, my leg thrown over his. I'm wound around him, and Ryder's wound around me.

It feels ... nice.

Carefully, and a little regretfully, I pull my hand from beneath the elastic. I take my time running my fingertips up the etched lines of his fantastic chest. Slowly, I detour back down his smooth body. When his head tips back with a quiet moan I decide I should probably stop pawing all over Daxdyn Riles like he's my own personal toy.

It takes several minutes, but I carefully unwind our limbs from each other and slip away from the most peaceful sleep I've had in five years.

I stare down at them from the foot of the bed and a smile rests against my lips. In my absence, Ryder has shifted closer to Daxdyn. His hand lays on Daxdyn's smooth stomach the same way it did mine. Daxdyn cradles Ryder's head with one hand and rests his other palm on Ryder's upper bicep.

My brows raise wondering just how close the two of them might really get. Instead of allowing them some privacy, I take a seat near the door and get comfortable for the show that is bound to break out at any moment.

I'm just throwing my leg over the side of the chair and slouching down when the door swings open.

A sharp pang jars through my stomach. I didn't lock the door last night.

They distracted me so much that I never locked the door behind us.

And yet, I slept peacefully.

Darrio's hard gaze softens as his brows raise. He looks from his friends and then, slowly, his attention pulls to me.

"I was only in the way," I say, shrugging my

shoulders at his incredulous look.

His eyes drop to the hard erections both men are sporting and he takes an intentional step back from them. He stands more in the hall now than in the room itself.

A woman in just her bra and underwear passes behind Darrio, and she looks carelessly our way before looking back down the hall. Her head flings back up, her eyes growing wide with interest at the sight within the room.

I stand, my hand slipping around Darrio's as I drag him inside and close the door swiftly behind him.

"You act like you've never seen two dicks in one place before." I say it to annoy him. I haven't had the opportunity to see something so amazing either, but it doesn't stop me from taunting him.

His serious eyes fall to me and he rakes his attention down my body. The look he always gives me makes my heart race. I'm still not entirely sure I'm not a masochist. Darrio doesn't look at me with desire. He looks at me like I disgust him and intrigue him all at once.

And for whatever reason it makes me smirk. It makes me want to get a rise out of him. It makes me want to give him a reason not to like me.

Or so I tell myself.

He licks his lips before looking away from me. A thundering sound accompanies his steps as he makes his way to the foot of the bed. With a hard thrust of his foot he bangs his boot against the bedframe, shaking it violently.

A wide stance fills his massive frame as he waits for them to flutter their pretty little eyes open.

Ryder actually pulls Daxdyn closer to him and buries his face into his neck.

Laughter rumbles through me, but I push it down out of fear of disturbing their intimate moment.

When the hard, straining length beneath Ryder's thin boxers grinds against Daxdyn's muscled thigh, I nearly clap with excitement.

Darrio doesn't share one bit of my lust-filled enthusiasm.

If I had to guess, I'd say it's probably the strength surrounding him that has Daxdyn raising his hands away from his friend's hard body. His hands are held above his head as if he's surrendering. He looks around the tangled sheets to find Ryder pressed sexually against his side.

"What the fuck, man?" He shoves at Ryder's arm that he was just caressing a moment ago.

Darrio looks back at me and the smallest smirk pulls at his full lips. That tingling feeling starts right back up in my stomach.

I practically roll my eyes at myself and my primal reaction to his attention.

Ryder's blue eyes flutter open, and he raises his lashes to look up at Daxdyn before shoving harshly away from him.

And here I thought their friendship could withstand close proximity, morning hard-ons.

"You ladies about ready to leave?" Darrio asks them, his smile growing with each passing second.

"I was actually starting to call them Thing One and Thing Two," I mention in a quiet tone. All eyes swing to me.

Laughter shakes through Darrio's chest and the sound of it makes a proud smile form on my lips.

Today's going to be a good day.

***

Ryder's sea blue gaze lands on me once more. It's the third time in twenty minutes. The soft cotton of his shirt brushes against my wrist as we walk. My fingers run through my long, dusty blonde hair, shading me from his suspicious glances.

What is he thinking?

A tired sigh slips from my lips. I'm almost done with this journey.

The sea is just up the bend. Dark, smoky clouds blanket the pale morning sky. I can almost taste the burnt smell of Juvar.

We're close to it. Close to the Hopeless city as well, I suppose.

Daxdyn had asked me to come with them. Could I really do that? It seems … impossible.

All my adult life I've only ever been a thief. I'm not special. I'm just human.

"You weren't born with the mark of the Hopeless?" I ask, tilting my head slightly toward Ryder.

His hands push into his pockets, bunching his wide shoulders together.

"No, I'm mixed; half fae, half human. My
112

mother was apparently fae. Sometimes the fae blood lies dormant. I could have lived my whole life as a simple human. Sometimes it manifests. The power of my blood changed, marring my body with this scar." He holds his arm out and I think about how similar his mark is to mine. "It's just like scar tissue, but once you enter the Hopeless realm it darkens with power. Once a fae enters the Hopeless realm, their energy surges and their true power awakens. They aren't truly fae until they enter the Hopeless realm."

From behind us, Darrio and Daxdyn talk among themselves about the soldier we ran into. The one walking around with Darrio's hand prints on his face now. The two of them chuckle and laugh about the ordeal. A smile pulls at my lips and I look back long enough for my eyes to meet Darrio's light gaze. Quickly I look away before our easy comradery ends with him calling me a 'fucking human' again.

"The twins, they're full blooded then?"

"Yeah, they were born into the Hopeless city. Their powers are a bit stronger than mine. They've had longer to train their abilities. But they took me in. Helped me understand what I was. I was never alone because of them." I glance to him. His strong jaw is tilted down as he watches his boots skim across the dry grass.

My heart warms thinking of the three of them as a family.

I wish I had that.

"Shit. We're here," Daxdyn says, his chest brushing against my back as we all come to an abrupt stop.

It's felt like an eternity has passed, but the black ocean that separates this safe land from the kingdom of Juvar is now right in front of me. The ocean would probably be beautiful if the sun could cast across it. Nothing but inky color shines within the depthless sea.

Dread sinks into me at just the sight of the drifting water. The waves crash against shore, pushing recklessly at it. An enormous ship is anchored at the coast. The ship makes my stomach sink even further.

Across the broad side of the glossy ship are the carefully written words The Noble Kingdom of Juvar.

It looks like a prison all on its own.

Two soldiers enter the only building in sight. The three fae make their way closer to that building, and my steps begin to slow. I fall back until I'm barely keeping up with them.

"Stay out here, we'll make some arrangements," Ryder tells me as all three of them enter the only building around for miles.

The building isn't one I'd willingly step foot in anyway. Jagged pieces of what once were the windows hang from wide openings in the brick structure. Ash taints every inch of it, shadowing it with a burnt and decayed look.

I lean against the wall, letting the char stain my clothes. Dark clouds and pollution cover the sky, shutting out the sunlight and any sign of the good mood I possessed from earlier this morning.

Two men in pressed uniforms descend the ship. My heart thrashes at the sight of them walking my way. It only takes a second for me to make up my mind. Stealthily, I slip into the building.

The door swings open with a shuddering, screeching sound. I flinch from the noise. Then, I come face to face with Daxdyn.

His posture tenses at the sight of me.

"You shouldn't be in here." His warm palms shove against my shoulders but, with a simple turn, I slip away from him. He isn't his brother. He doesn't manhandle me like his brother. Realistically, I don't believe Daxdyn has the aggression in him to wrestle me to the dirty floor over something he barely seems to care about.

He watches me with interest as I skim my index finger along a tall table. Dust clings to my fingertips. Opened cardboard boxes litter the floors and wooden table tops. Tattered envelopes of every size are scattered haphazardly in every corner. The letters USPS graces every one of the forgotten parcels.

"They told you to wait outside. If Darrio finds you here, he won't be happy."

I almost roll my eyes. Is Darrio ever really happy?

"Perhaps I'll tell him his brother snuck me in." I look up at him from beneath my long lashes. Firmly, my lips pull together.

His mouth opens with a slight smile. "Do you always have something terrible waiting on the tip of your tongue to be said?"

At the mention of my tongue, he takes his time crossing the messy room. His fingers splay across the tabletop, an inch away from my own. The lean muscles of his chest are emphasized by his thin white shirt that's stretched across it.

"It could just be that I'm a terrible person,

Daxdyn." The crooked smile on his lips causes me to breathe out his name on an uneven breath.

"I don't believe that." The warmth of his palm skims along my jaw as he carefully pushes back my long blonde hair. "You saved us from that tower. I thought I'd die up there, and you saved me." A look of wonder gleams in his gray eyes.

The screeching of the door breaks the trance in an instant.

"Shit." He shoves me by the back of my head until I'm crouched down. From below the table, past mounds of boxes and crinkled papers, I can barely see Darrio's wide shoulders spanning the doorframe.

Why can't I be in here? Because I'm a girl? Because they think they're in charge? Or are they hiding the arrangements they are making here?

My teeth grind together just thinking about what their petty reasoning could be.

"What are you doing? We're almost done already."

Daxdyn tilts his head down and gives me a long, hard look before releasing his fingers from my hair and giving his brother a smooth smile.

"I think you were right, shouldn't have ate that food at the whore house yesterday." His palm runs over his stomach.

My eyes narrow on him.

He might be a better liar than I am.

I guess we'll see.

Kneeling on the dusty floor at his feet, my fingertips push up his thigh. He tenses from my touch but never breaks eye contact with Darrio.

"You need a minute or what?" Darrio's voice holds a hint of annoyance.

My palm pushes demandingly against the center of his jeans. Rough fabric and a noticeable hardness is all that can be felt. He shifts, his boots scuffing the tile. I rub more until the harsh sound of his voice clearing makes me smile.

With a quick flick of my wrist the zipper lowers with ease, and smooth skin meets my eager fingers.

My heart pounds, and I watch his face closely as I take him in my hand and begin to roll my wrist slowly up and then down.

I really am a terrible person.

"I—" Daxdyn murmurs before clasping his hands together. "I'm gonna need a minute." The clipped words grind out.

Darrio curls his lips at his brother's odd behavior. I lean into Daxdyn's warm body, pulling at his hard length until his sensitive, smooth skin presses to my full lips. Daxdyn slowly lowers his eyes and shoots me a single, desperate look. Something similar to pain and worry fills his face.

Holding his beautiful gaze, I swipe my tongue across the tip. My lips wrap around him, and I lower them until his hardness hits the back of my throat.

He groans and leans his weight onto the table top, his hands still clasped as he hangs his head low. In a rushed movement, his fingers thread through the back of my hair. Faster, I move against him, my hands gripping his thighs as I hold him to me.

"I'll be outside. You look like shit." Darrio's confused voice echoes through the small room.

Daxdyn's teeth clench as he nods carelessly to his brother.

The moment the door screeches closed, Daxdyn leans back against the brick wall, his head tipping up to the ceiling. Tightly, his fingers grip my locks as he guides my mouth down his throbbing dick.

"*Fuck*." The word's a rasping whisper that makes my thighs clench together. I suck harder just as warmth slips across my tongue. Every muscle in his body tenses.

When I press a final kiss to his slick skin, he loosens his grip on my now tangled hair.

Slowly, his back slides down the concrete wall until we're eye to eye. His hands still hold my head. Wide, gray eyes look at me with a mischievous glint in them. I swallow hard and my tongue slips out and licks across my bottom lip.

"You're," his thumb brushes the outline of my mouth, tingling energy right through me, "not at all what I thought you'd be."

I want to reach out and touch him too; run my fingers up the smooth edge of his strong jaw.

But I don't move an inch for fear the emotions in me will break and come falling out of my tightly closed heart.

As much as I don't want to, I like Daxdyn. It's a reckless feeling that shakes through me. It worries me. Caring about someone is dangerous. Caring about someone as careless as Daxdyn is asking for trouble.

The buckle of his jeans clasps once again as he zips up his pants. Then he takes my hand in his, spreading warmth through me from the weirdly intimate feel of his hand in mine. For once, I don't object. I let him lead me from the room.

When we step foot outside, I keep my place directly behind him, hiding in his shadow from the guards that might be lurking.

We wait for only a moment before Darrio and Ryder join us. Their eyes fall to Daxdyn's possessive hand on mine.

His fingers slip away from me and he doesn't give me a second look.

"So?" Daxdyn asks as he raises his palms from his sides with impatience.

Darrio cocks a dark brow at his brother.

"So we leave at dawn. The guards inside said the ship is heading back to Juvar tomorrow morning."

We.

He definitely means them.

"And I suppose, I'll be taking my payment

now."

All three of them pin me with a look that makes me shift on my feet.

"We've never been to Juvar. Hell, the former prince himself hasn't seen it in decades." Darrio gestures to Ryder. "Take us to the gates and we'll pay you."

"She doesn't have to do that," Daxdyn says.

Is he defending me?

It feels odd to have someone stick up for me. It makes me … uncomfortable.

"We had a deal. I brought you to the shore. That is as far as I go."

I certainly am not stepping foot on a Noble ship.

This is why I wasn't allowed inside. They were arranging their departure with the enemy.

"He's right, Kara. We need you." Ryder's pleading gaze only makes me angrier. "Come to the kingdom with us and I'll pay you double."

Anger burns rapidly through my tight chest.

"You don't even know my fucking price." The

words seethe through clenched teeth. My fists shake at my sides.

I should have known better than to trust them. I need to go. Now. This is dangerous. They're going to get me killed.

Or worse.

"Fine," I grind out. My lips press so tightly together it hurts. I can't look any of them in the eye. The dry dirt holds my attention.

"Fine?" Darrio repeats like a broken clock that can go fuck itself for all I care.

"Okay. We better make camp then," Ryder says uneasily. His eyes bore into me but I refuse to look at him.

He's a liar. They all are.

First thing tomorrow morning, they'll be sailing away from me.

And I'll never see them again.

Chapter Eleven
An Opportunity

With defiance, I glare up at the heavy moon. It looms wide in the sky, taking up too much of the beautiful, starry heavens.

Their snores lull softly around me.

A pleasing sound.

The feeling of achievement swirls within me, and I slowly stand. The thin blanket slips from my poised body, falling to the dirt without a sound. My gaze drifts over Darrio and Daxdyn. They lie on their sides facing the forest. Ryder lies closest to the small, fuming fire with his back to me as well.

I smile at them; at the sound of their tired breaths.

They'd be cute if I cared for them at all.

An indifference fills me as I shrug my

shoulders at the thought and move away on soundless steps. My heart pounds as I skim through the shadows, away from the three men who I wish I could trust. I wish them nothing but the best in life, really, I do—just without me in it.

The heaviness of the sword bumps against my thigh as I trail along the enormous waterfront. As if I'd risk my life to sail on a Nobel ship and cross these waters with men I barely know.

I can't believe they believed me.

A smirk catches my lips as I roll my eyes at their pathetically naive minds.

Then he tackles me. For the second time since we've met.

The wind is knocked out of me as Darrio's rigid body rushes mine. He grips my waist, strong arms holding me tightly. I shove against him, breathing hard as I push at his shoulders.

I stumble and he pulls me into him, his warmth surrounding me.

He does nothing but stare at me for a moment. Light shines against his beautiful eyes. My heart skips a beat from the unfiltered look he's giving me.

Then my fist connects with his strong jaw and I slip out of his grasp.

His teeth clench together. He reaches for me once more but I push him off.

Warm hands brush around my hips and he tackles me to the ground. We fumble until we both fall into the cold water of the ocean.

"Oh, my Gods above!" I seethe, my shoulders hunching as a chill stings into my skin. "You asshole." I shove against his slick arm once more.

He wastes no time as he lifts me from the sea, water dripping down my body as he throws me over his shoulder.

The way his fingers skim my flesh along my lower back sets me on fire.

I cannot believe he's doing this.

"Darrio, put me down," I demand in a weak whisper as we get closer to our camp.

"Why, so you can ditch us again?" His voice skips a little as my fists beat against his wide shoulders. "They trusted you. You're nothing more than a selfish little brat."

My lips curl at his description. Outrage burns through me.

126

I open my mouth to correct him but nothing comes out.

I come before anyone else. It's been that way since I was sixteen. Me and me alone.

Selfish.

Yes.

"What did you expect?" I hiss.

He sits me down. My damp, pale hair clings to my jaw line.

His lips part just as I start to unbutton my pants. The line between his brows smooths as he follows my movements. Without hesitancy, I kick angrily out of my boots and shimmy out of the drenched jeans.

"What the hell are you doing?" He shifts nervously, his steely eyes darting to his brother's sleeping form before coming back to me.

"I'll freeze if I stay in wet clothes." I say it slowly to him as if he's a child. "People die of pneumonia. Did you know that?"

With confusion-filled eyes, he stares at me.

"That's not how humans get pneumonia ..."

Ignoring his reply, I turn away from him and his reasoning.

I'd take off my soaked vest as well, but I'm not wearing a bra. I don't want poor Darrio to have a fucking heart attack.

Gently, I lay out my only pair of jeans near the warm fire. A tangle of white locks meets my fingertips as I try to dry my thick hair a little.

With a short stick, I stoke the meager embers into a small fire. A minute passes. My gaze clings to the flickering flames.

I shoot Darrio a look of annoyance before I take my place on my shabby pallet once again. The thin blanket does little to warm me. I shift even closer to the heat.

Lying on my back once more, I realize Darrio still stands as he was; staring at me with his lips set into a tight line.

"Swallow down your ego and take your pants off already. I won't peek. I promise."

It's a lie and we both know it.

I haven't seen a man naked in almost a year. I've never seen a man as gorgeous as Darrio naked in my entire life.

Never let an opportunity pass you by Lady Ivory used to tell me.

I won't, Lady Ivory, I won't.

My fingers thread through my hair as I lean up on my elbow to give him my fullest attention.

A smile almost touches his lips before he pushes it back down. He turns fully to me, and my heart races as my eyes widen.

Is he serious?

The ever-scowling Darrio has a playful side?

His hands reach slowly behind him, pulling at the neck of his long sleeve shirt. My lips part as he lifts the traitorous shirt from his body.

With torturously slow movements, the shirt rises from his abdomen. Hard lines cut into a v along his hips. A light trail of dark hair disappears into the top of his low-slung jeans. Jagged scar tissue skims his side demanding my attention just as much as his defined chest does. Black ink swirls across his wide shoulders and reaches down to the mark of the Hopeless on his left arm. The intricate tattoos stand out against the white, twisting scars that adorn his hard body.

His long hair is ruffled when he finally pulls

the shirt off. The firelight glints in his eyes. For once I'm thankful for the moonlight, the firelight, all the light that graces his gorgeous body just for me.

The two of us stare at one another. It's the first time a few minutes have passed without one of us saying something foul to the other.

It's almost nice not hating him.

His fingers begin unbuttoning his pants.

Okay, it's more than nice.

It's fantastic.

He doesn't look at me as he pushes his jeans down his hips and kicks off his boots. He shoves his clothes in a crumbled pile near the flames. In just his boxers, he turns his back on me and walks to his pallet, ten feet from mine, and lies down.

He stares daggers at me from across the fire. Wide eyes watch my every move.

Playtime is over. I'm his untrusted companion once more.

I doubt he'll sleep a wink tonight.

Cold hair clings to my slight shoulders and I shuffle a little closer to the fire.

Darrio cocks his head quickly, getting a better view of me.

"Calm down," I hiss, "I'm just cold. I'm not making a run for it, I swear."

He settles back into his blanket.

"Not right now anyway." I smirk to myself, slightly pleased to see him scowling again.

Again, he cocks his head at me and we hold glares for several seconds. His jaw tics, and he stands. He jerks his blanket from the ground and his feet scuff angrily against the dirt. With long strides, he makes his way toward me. He throws the blanket near my side and lies down. I jump when his warm arm wraps around my cold stomach.

"What are you doing?" My spine is stiff against his chest.

"Making sure we don't lose our guide."

"By cuddling me? You're fighting back with cuddles?" I keep my eyes on the flickering flames, refusing to look at him as he holds me.

"I'm not a cuddler." His breath fans against my neck, a tingling sensation follows its wake.

"This feels suspiciously like cuddling, Rio."

"I hate when you call me that."

A smirk curves my lips. I'm going to have to say that's a victory for the night. It was a good night all in all. I got to see Darrio almost naked, my clothes are partially clean, and now I'm surrounded by warmth as I sleep.

In comparison to my normal nights alone on the streets, tonight's been decent.

My legs shift against his. A constricting feeling begins to build in my chest from my lack of space. I guess I'm not used to being so close to someone. It makes me more restless. I wiggle a little, trying to find comfort on the ground with the weight of Darrio pressing into me.

Then I still, my eyes going wide as I feel his hard dick low against my back.

"Stop. Moving." His gravelly voice demands into my hair.

My lips part with a surprised smile. A warm feeling spreads through me, my heart skipping slightly.

I'm not sure why the dirty thoughts begin to fly through my mind, but they do.

With intent, I roll my hips; shifting a little

more. His large hand splays wide across my abdomen.

"I said stop moving." It's a plea almost; gruff and rasping.

My thighs clench from just the sound of his voice against my neck.

His voice always sinks right into me, and right now it seems to drive deep into my chest.

Slow movements fill my hips as I grind against him. His head dips low, leaning into my neck. Warm, heavy breaths kiss my shoulder blade.

"Zakara." His whisper soaks into me, sinking right to my core.

All of the terrible things we've said to one another have led to this.

Rough fingers skim down my hips, over my underwear. He cups me between my legs and my lips part.

My eyes fling open, assessing our surroundings. The other two men still face the woods. Their snores are barely heard over my gasping breath.

For a second, my mind tries to think this through. I try desperately to think through the haze in my mind to find an ulterior motive that Darrio might have for getting me in this position.

Could he hurt me?

Steal from me?

What does he gain?

His lips press lightly against the curve of my neck. He shifts against me. Swiftly he pushes my underwear to the side and I feel his smooth length against me.

All logical thought slips from my mind.

I arch against his chest, my leg shifting to accommodate him.

A low groan filters from his lips and onto my neck as he pushes against my sensitive skin. Slowly, his dick sinks into me. I bite my lip hard, and a long, muted breath escapes me. His hand comes back up to my hip and my fingers grip his wrist as he unhurriedly slides deep into me. Sharp teeth sink into my shoulder and my moan matches his.

Our pleasure is silenced. A mixture of anxiety and excitement swirls dangerously within my chest. The rasping sound of my breath is all that can be heard. I can't look away from Daxdyn and

Ryder for fear that I'll be caught screwing the one person I thought I hated.

Shamelessly, I meet his hard thrusts. My back arches against him, finding a perfect and unhurried rhythm.

Gods above, does he have rhythm.

Painfully, his fingers dig into my hipbone as he guides my every move. His hand skims low until he pushes aside my panties once more, his fingers rough against my flesh.

I gasp when his fingertips push against my clit. My eyes flutter closed, and I moan as I shift against his talented fingers.

At the sound of my unfiltered appreciation, Darrio's other hand slips beneath my head. Warm fingers brush against my parted lips as he shoves his hand over my mouth, muffling my voice. The quieted moans seem to fuel him on. Harder, he drives his dick into me. His fingers roll against me, building a restless energy low in my stomach.

I raise my hand and reach back for him. I run my fingers through his dark hair, pulling at the roots.

My thighs shake and, with another long stroke, I come hard around him. With my eyes clenched tightly closed, I open my mouth and bite down rigidly on his fingers.

A humming groan tingles into my neck, his beard scraping against my skin. With another jerking motion, he stills against me. Sweat clings to our bodies, not an inch of space separates us. Slowly, he lowers his hand from my mouth.

The thrashing sound of my heart is all I can focus on. I open my eyes. The firelight greets me. The other two men are still sleeping soundly. Nothing's changed. All is the same.

Neither of us move. We don't speak. There's nothing to say.

He slips himself from me, shifting away. The tingling feeling still spikes through my veins. For a moment, his warm hand holds my hip. A gentle kiss skims across my shoulder before he turns away from me, lying flat on his back.

"Goodnight, Kara."

Tension fills my body at the sound of my name. It's the first time he's ever actually said my name and it causes an odd feeling to drift through me.

And yet, nothing's changed.

Chapter Twelve

The Beauty in Scars

I do sleep. Very comfortably actually. Just before the cloudy sunlight touches the horizon, Darrio's lips skim my shoulder, sending a shiver all through my body.

My lashes slowly flutter open. His steely gaze holds mine. There's an animalistic look in his eyes. It's tinged with confusion and want. I know he'll never ask me to tell him my feelings.

And that's good. Because I have no idea what they are.

His brother was right; Darrio and I are the same. He just expresses his anger while I misplace mine. Rough hands meet my abdomen, brushing across my ribs. My thighs clench together as a shiver runs across my flesh

"Did I hurt you?" he whispers, his attention shifting toward the dry ground.

The two of us are in uncharted territory. We were so good at hating each other. It's apparently hard to know how to be civil to one another.

I shake my head at him.

Ever so lightly, his fingers skim across my ribs. I feel the tingle of his magic burn lightly through me. My eyes flutter from his surprisingly gentle touch.

My gaze shifts, trying to capture his every move.

I'll need to get some Silphium when we get to the coast. The pretty plant that Saint's Inn always has in high supply flashes through my mind. As beautiful as a little fire fae baby would be, I'm not at all prepared for a smaller, angrier version of Darrio running around.

"Where'd this one come from?" he asks me in a gravelly voice, pulling me from my thoughts.

I lick my lips, my gaze pulling away from his to notice the pale scar running along my side.

"I got caught stealing from a drunk when I was seventeen." A fond smile pulls at my lips. "I don't steal from drunks anymore. Very often."

He smirks at me as his fingers continue tracing

along my body. Making me crazy.

"And this one?" He skims the side of my neck, his thumb brushing over my jaw.

I've never talked with him like this. I don't know if I've ever spoke with anyone like this.

"A man tried to take more than I offered once." The smile falls from my lips as I remember the first person I ever killed.

Darrio's brows raise high.

Carefully, as if he isn't sure he'll actually do it, he leans into me and presses a gentle kiss to the imperfect line against the base of my neck. My eyes flutter closed as he seals a new memory to the scar.

Lady Ivory always said I'd be perfect if I wasn't flawed by so many scars. If I was more of a lady and less of thief. I always told her she'd be perfect if she wasn't a whore. And we'd laugh, both of us ignoring what life had given us.

"You're ... more than just your scars. You know that, right?"

I nod, my eyes narrowing on his worried face. It's a weird look he's giving me.

He pauses, as if it's hard for him to admit what

he's about to say to me. "You're more than just beautiful."

Again, I nod slowly.

I don't know how we got here. Somewhere during our journey, I went from being the *fucking human* to being beautiful in his eyes.

I haven't decided if he's still an asshole or not. At the moment he isn't, but just give it time and I'm sure we'll fall right back into the bickering hate we held before.

His icy gaze dances across my features.

"Never forget that."

He glances to my lips. We've had sex, and yet, he hasn't tried to kiss me again. A tingling feeling returns low in my stomach as I remember the way his lips felt against mine.

Stiffly he nods, breaking his attention away from my mouth before he pulls away from me. My stomach sinks hard as he stands and starts to pull on his pants.

The tides have changed. I can't say that I have. I feel it though. I'm different. Because of these three ridiculous fae, I'm different now.

And I'm terrified of what that means.

Chapter Thirteen
The Kingdom

The glaring, diluted sunlight lashes out at me. I narrow my gaze on the horizon. This ship, the sea, and the growing anxiety within my chest has tortured me for two hours now.

We glide through the ocean at a snail's pace on the Nobel ship. I have mixed feelings; wanting to finally arrive in the kingdom and also wanting to never step foot on its terrible land.

There was once a neighboring island, that's now been swallowed up by the ocean, that was fondly named Fire Island. That name feels right. That name fits Juvar perfectly.

Daxdyn watches me while I keep my attention focused on the shore that I know will come into view at any moment.

"What will it be like, the city of the Hopeless?" All I can think about is how much I want it to be different from this world. Separate from this hell that I've grown up in.

Salty ocean air chills my flesh and I pull my arms around myself. It's almost here. I can feel it. It's a hell I never wanted to return to. It's like the land is pushing against the sea, not the other way around.

"It's different. Beautiful. Not at all like your world. It's ... just different. You'll be different there too," Daxdyn says in a whisper. His attention is held on me, but I can't bring myself to look at him. "Your powers can't awaken until you've been Hopelessly reborn." He clasps his hands against the railing. Daxdyn's still oblivious to the land up ahead. He doesn't feel it the way I do. It isn't calling him home.

My shoulders tense just thinking about it. Am I really what they say I am? What if it's all just a lie? What if I'm not special at all? What if my father died for nothing?

For hours, the guards of this ship have looked at us skeptically. It's a plotting look that makes me want to risk my life jumping over the railing right now.

What did Ryder promise them for allowing us passage on their ship?

Currently, two guards stand only a few yards away. They're speaking in low voices and their attention is held on us. The weight of their gazes are pressing into me; setting me on edge. My nerves tingle through me, but still I hold a look of self-assurance safely in place.

We were told we were offered safe passage to the kingdom.

But I always know a lie when I hear one.

Darrio glances to me out of the corner of his steely eyes. It's like he can feel my anxiety despite my neutral expression. Hesitantly, he takes a single step closer to me. I feel his strong chest brushing lightly against my back.

If he and I were different people, Darrio might wrap his arms around me, and I'd lean into him. He'd tell me it'd be alright in the quietest of whispers. And I'd believe him.

If we were different people.

But we're not.

Daxdyn's simple happiness falls away, turning into confusion as he lifts his hands to catch the light pieces of gray flakes drifting through the air.

"Is that," slowly his brows pull together,

"snow?"

It isn't. I wish it was. I wish the ash falling from the sky was simply cold weather instead of the destruction of the city up ahead. I can't bring myself to correct Daxdyn. It's easier just to ignore the pale ash that's clinging to my hair and lashes. It brushes across my tightly closed lips, pushing to seep into my body.

Ryder leans into my side, his shoulder bumping mine. His attention burns across my body in a demanding way. My gaze pulls from the lapping waves of the dark ocean, and I look at him.

A simple, easy smile is all he gives me. It makes my heart thunder to life.

He glances away for only a second. Then the happiness slips from his lips.

"What the hell is that?" His eyes narrow on the horizon.

I know what it is before I even turn to look.

Fire billows up into the heavens from the destroyed city up ahead. Impossibly steep, dark buildings claw at the gray and blue sky. Rods of steel hang like talons from the remains of old skyscrapers. The tops of the structures are jagged, fallen away over time. They teeter with the strong winds of the ocean as if the world is pulling at the remainder of the lives that live here. The cities are worse, much worse than the smaller villages.

The cities depended on the fae more and the remnants of powerful magic still lingers in the air here. It's dangerous and a constant state of combustion.

But humans cling to these deadly shores in hopes that the Hopeless will return to us.

Magic no longer supports our world like it once did.

A charred and broken society is all that's left in its wake. The blackened and burning city reflects in Ryder's beautiful gaze. I might always want to see this terrible world through his eyes.

"That, my Prince, is your kingdom."

The End

A.K. Koonce

The Hopeless Series continues! Book two, Hopeless Kingdom is now available on preorder!

A.K. Koonce

Also by A.K. Koonce

The Mortals and Mystics Series

Fate of the Hybrid, Prequel

When Fate Aligns, Book one

When Fate Unravels, Book two

When Fate Prevails, Book three

The Resurrection Series

Resurrection Island, Book one

The Royal Harem Series

The Hundred Year Curse

The Curse of the Sea

The Legend of the Cursed Princess

A.K. Koonce

About A.K. Koonce

A.K. Koonce is a USA Today bestselling author. She's mom by day and a fantasy and paranormal romance writer by night. She keeps her fantastical stories in her mind on an endless loop while she tries her best to focus on her actual life and not that of the spectacular, but demanding, fictional characters who always fill her thoughts.

Printed in Great Britain
by Amazon